Mister Sugar

The Bachelors of Dream Heights

Olivia Monroe

Published by DTM Publishing, LLC, 2022.

MISTER SUGAR

First edition. January 2, 2022.

ISBN: 979-8201250942

Written by Olivia Monroe.

Chapter 1: Office With A View

For the last three years, I focused solely on the business. Like my dad Frank, I intended to be a strong leader. If I couldn't bring Whitmer Real Estate more business, I would be a certified failure ... until the housing crisis.

Yeah, turns out California isn't a great place to be the CEO of a real estate agency. Work has been crawling at a snail's pace and, even though I want to be the human version of a city on a hill for this agency, the market won't let me. Because of that, my mind's been wandering off a lot. As it stands, the agency will survive this slow period. But as for myself, I don't know. Dad always encouraged me to work my ass off, and I get the feeling that he's laughing at his own past advice these days — the man is enjoying his retirement as a millionaire who will probably make more in stocks alone over this next decade than what the average American will make in a lifetime. And he's back on the dating scene after years of not so much as touching a woman. I'm beginning to see the appeal.

At work, there are about five women out of the fifteen employees stationed on the same floor as me in our office building. Three of these women are attractive, in my opinion, and out of the three, two are single. I haven't felt the need to date since my junior year of college, when I fell in love for a total of three months, then split off as soon as I smelled a growing dependency between us. When your parents divorce early enough in your life — mine did just before my ninth birthday — that can really mess with your "connectability," so to speak. Women call it a fear of commitment. I call it a safety precaution.

But the more I look over my paper-littered desk and through the glass door that separates my office from their cubicles, I can't help but contemplate what it would be like to date one of the two bachelorettes. I'm a little ashamed to admit that I had one of them, Tonya Jefferson, move from the front of the big white room — near the elevator entrance — over to the back where my office is *just so I could watch her as she worked*. Obviously, I framed this at the time as a promotion, since she now sits by some wide windows that give her an A+ view of the Pacific. She's still none the wiser, and sits beside the lovely Mariah Chase who frequently defies the office dress code, to my pleasure.

Oh well. I might be the CEO, but I don't have the courage to pursue them at the moment. It would be inappropriate of me to do so, because I'm their boss. Unless one of them pursues me, I'm better off just forgetting them. HR is no joke.

My cell phone vibrates in my pocket. A personal call? Must be Dad. I reach into my black slacks and pull out my silver touch-screen phone that cost me over a thousand dollars. It's new, so it's gotta be worth the investment ... I think.

Answering the call after a quick confirming glance at the caller ID I say, "what's up, Dad?"

"Exciting stuff, Marlon." Frank Whitmer addresses me in the cheerful well-off-man-in-his-seventies tone that he didn't start using until his retirement some years ago.

Before then, he was always curt. Unless you were doing him a favor, he would basically tell you to fuck off. Nowadays, you would have to have known the man to imagine this. It's like I lost my father and got a new, shinier one. Only instead of paying a thousand dollars for this upgrade, I pay him in my labor and financial success.

"What kind of exciting stuff?" I ask. What would excite this old man so much that he needs to tell me about it?

Leaning back in my chair, I spin around to face the window behind me. The sight of the Pacific relaxes me, and the only thing that would make this office better would be if I could open the window just a crack to let in the sound of waves washing up onto the shore, shrieking seagulls, and if I could just breathe in the briny smell of the ocean. I guess the traffic on the streets below might take away from the beach sounds and smells, though.

Dad says giddily, "I'm having dinner tonight — with a wonderful lady."

I sigh and shake my head, though he obviously can't see me. "I'm happy for you. Have fun."

"Don't think I'm calling just to brag, Lonnie. This is a big deal for me. We've been seeing each other for a while."

"Oh, so it's not a new girl. What's her name again? I think you mentioned it once over the phone. Is it North? Leah? Natasha ...?"

"Natalie," he answers with an air of disappointment. "Anyway, I want you at dinner tonight, at my place. It'll be great. You'll see."

"Dinner? I can get behind that." I haven't met this Natalie my dad's been seeing. It's weird to admit it, since we had been working close to each other since I graduated with my business degree from UCLA, but my dad and I talk primarily over the phone these days. "What will we be having?"

"It's a surprise. Just come at six. Will you be there?"

"Obviously. I haven't had a dinner meeting scheduled for the last five months, so my nights are free."

We say a farewell, and see you later. He hangs up first. Putting my phone back in my pocket, I spin toward my desk and get back to long, boring work.

Chapter 2: My Dad Loves A Gold-digger

Later in the evening I drive up to his mansion in a gated community full of other kempt mansions. I'm almost jealous, but my house is about as large as any one of these. The only difference is I'm not living behind a huge metal fence.

Pulling into Dad's driveway, I park my Mercedes beside his and get out of my vehicle. I see him open the door and wave for me to come inside. The man's lost a lot of weight and hair with age, but he still has a fair amount of wavy white strands — they're just further back on his head now. He wears a casual but expensive outfit like I do. I learned my sense of style from him, after all. Plaid button-up with silky fabric and complimentary designer slacks. Of course, this outfit wouldn't be complete without the traditional polished leather shoes and a gold Rolex watch.

"Come in; meet Natalie," Dad says, placing his hand on my back as we go into his pristine home and make our way through a white-painted hallway, adorned by ornate plates from around the world. We enter the dining room, which features a large oak table, a crystalline chandelier, and a series of windows that open up to the tall trees surrounding his home. It isn't on the beach like Whitmer Real Estate, but it's still heavenly.

The only thing that sticks out to me when I get into the dining room, which already smells sublime thanks to the home-cooked barbecue set out before us, is *her*. She says in a surprised but pleasant voice, "Hi! I'm Natalie Green," and gets up to hug me. I don't hug her back, even though I want to when those fair, slender arms wrap around me. She's absurdly beautiful, but I can't let my mind wander off on tangents about how she looks. The smell of her perfume hits me — she smells like lavender and vanilla — and I have to hold my arms down at my sides to avoid feeling her up.

It's embarrassing! How did Dad catch such a fine-ass fish? I swear to God, between us two men from different generations, I'm the one who's always a step behind. Just by the feel of her big, round breasts on my chest, I know I would have picked her out of a lineup of beauties to make her my girlfriend, ten times out of ten. Somehow Dad beat me to it.

Once she lets go, I just take a seat across from her and where my father's plate sits. He joins us at the table, acting like everything is totally normal. But Natalie's pretty blue eyes take on a gleam of insecurity; her romantic red, doll-like lips purse at me.

She must know that I'm taking her in. I can't help it! Why would someone so young be here with my dad, and why does she wear a diamond-encrusted gold ring on her left index finger? She has on a light, flowery dress that reveals a good portion of her sizable breasts — my heart races when I think about how they felt against me just a moment ago — and when I quickly peek beneath the table, I can see that she wears brown sandals with straps that wind up halfway to her knees. Her plate has three BBQ ribs on it, and is mostly salad. Her straight, long hair is about the same color as withered grass.

It just isn't fair — I'll have to be careful not to think about her naked on my bed, to avoid the embarrassment of a hard-on outside the privacy of my own home. But it's also strange. Too strange for me not to question her motives.

"Before we get into any news," Dad says, picking up a fork and a knife, "I just want to say that I'm happy we're all here together. I cooked all this meat for tonight. Put my heart into it."

Natalie places her delicate hand on his broad, once very muscular shoulder. I see that she's painted her fingernails an orangey red. The way her soft face looks at my father makes me sick. What does this woman think she's doing, getting with a man three times her age?

"Thanks for cooking, Dad," I say to him.

Natalie echoes me with: "Yeah! This is amazing, Daddy."

I nearly choke. I haven't even eaten anything yet.

Dad wraps an arm around Natalie and, leaning in with his wrinkly face, he gives her a big kiss on the lips. How is this natural?

She's gotta be taking advantage of him for his money. She looks like she's fresh out of college!

What are you up to, Natalie Green?

"We're engaged," Dad says about twenty minutes into dinner, which primarily consisted of small talk. "In a few months, we'll be getting married — in Hawaii! Can you believe it? We want the ceremony to take place on a volcano."

"Won't you have trouble climbing to the top?" I ask, thinking practically as I try not to express my outrage at this ridiculous scenario.

What the hell is Frank Whitmer doing with a woman like Natalie? She laughs at my joke, but it's not much of a joke at all. He also chuckles, not seeming to get the picture.

"Forgive me if I'm wrong for bringing it into question again, since we've already introduced each other ..." I dab my lips with a napkin. "But what are you doing with a twenty-four-year-old?"

Dad catches onto my sober tone, but seems to dismiss it immediately. "I should be asking *you*: what *aren't* you doing with a twenty-four-year-old?"

Natalie sits back in her chair, petite shoulders hunching forward a little. Part of me empathizes with her discomfort, but I have enough respect for a woman who's been through higher education to make the assumption that she knows just how suspicious any major age-gap relationship makes people. She should expect me, the man's son, to wonder about her intentions.

I start to consider my own thinking, however. Dad knows that he might be susceptible to gold-diggers at his age and financial status; he may have decided in this case that he was willing to take a risk.

"If I can say something," Natalie starts, not sounding as shy or uncomfortable as her posture suggests.

Dad nods at her, encouraging her to talk, which she does while staring at me, as if she's challenging me to a battle of some verbal variety. *Well, Natalie, I'll show you who's on top.*

She says, "Frank is the best, most supportive and enthusiastic man I've ever encountered. I grew up around men: brothers, my dad and my uncles. I went to school surrounded by boys, and I was in plenty of clubs with young men in college. But *none of them* are like your father." She reaches for his hand on the table, and he holds onto hers like she's a precious gem. "None of them have his wisdom or his *joie de vivre.*"

"Maybe I'm cynical, but you studied art: anyone would assume that you're strapped for cash."

Natalie gives me a displeased look and says, "I also studied infrastructure and could easily get a job. Obviously, it helps that Frank has money. But that's not why I'm with him."

Dad adds, frowning, "she's right, Marlon. Now, I respect you and love you. You're my son. But if you start questioning my *fiancé's* integrity, I'll have to ask you to leave."

I can't believe my old man. How can he buy into Natalie's "love" talk? He divorced the woman who swore until she took her last goddamn breath that she loved him! With a grunt, I stand up and say, "funny you should say that. Turns out I have to go."

"What?" He blinks in confusion, also standing up. Natalie copies him like a shadow. "Marlon, I'm not saying I don't want you here. I'm saying you need to be respectful of my soon-to-be wife! We're engaged!"

"I saw the ring on her finger," I shout from the hallway, so they hear me. "I'll call you tomorrow, but I'm done for tonight! Thanks for the dinner!"

I leave the house and get into my Mercedes, feeling my heart race in my chest. My doubts about their relationship are only stronger now that Dad says they're engaged. As his son, I should do him the favor of looking into ...

Natalie Green, graduate of California State University, class of 2022.

Chapter 3: Invitation To The Condo

I hadn't lied to my dad the night before. The very next day, I called him during my lunch break to tell him what I was up to. We started that conversation off with an awkward question about how each of us was enjoying the sunshine, then I got to work questioning him based on my findings from last night.

"What do you know about Natalie, Dad?"

He sounded miffed on the other end of the line. "I know what I know, Marlon. What's this all about? You storm outta my house and now you call me on the phone like you didn't make an ass of yourself!"

"I'm sorry about that, Dad," I said honestly. I hadn't intended to make an ass of myself; I only meant to reveal the obvious motive Ms. Green had to be romantic with my father. "But look, I'm just trying to help. You know? I'm your son. I care. And you're all I have, since Mom's gone."

"You're an adult, Marlon. Why not find yourself a wife, so I'm not the only person in your life?"

"How can I do that if I'm worried about your relationship?"

"Figure it out. You're a grown man, son."

I chuckled to myself, closing my eyes and shaking my head. "Dad, she just wants your money. You've been duped! Yeah, she's got her degrees; she hasn't done anything *wrong* on the books, but she could easily get a job and she hasn't, now has she? Don't you think that's strange?"

My dad just sighed. Then, after a long moment, he said, "I know all about that. She's an honest girl, if you just get to know her. Speaking of which, despite how rude you were at dinner last night, I want to give you the opportunity to *know you're wrong*. I'm inviting you to the condo."

The condo? Goddamn! That's a nice place with a perfect ocean view, pools, hot tubs, two Tiki bars for each side of the long line of condominiums ... if I wanted to get married, I wouldn't hate doing it on the docks out over the water. The place is clean and breezy, with shockingly minimal traffic to gunk up the air with exhaust and sounds of heavy motors. Two nights costs what I would make in a year. Not exactly affordable, according to my bank account.

"I'll pay for the whole thing," Dad continues. "Three nights by the water. Maybe I'm the idiot for wanting my young fiancé to get along with my grown-up son, but that's how I feel: I want you two to get along. Obviously, she won't be filling any sort of a mother role. I would never ask that of either of you. I just want my family, small as it is, to be happy. Can you play along for three nights, Marlon? You get your own room; even the balcony will be split in two, so you'll have privacy. Hell, you oughta invite a lady to join you. I'm paying for everything, so won't you come? Give her a chance, Marlon."

"Oh, all right. You know I can't turn that down...I want you to be happy too."

The call ends. I look across from my desk and spot the two beautiful ladies across from my office. I suppose I could call one of them into my office and ask them to go on a business trip with me ... Maybe offer a pay raise if she says yes? But I can't take them both, as much as I might want to. I also can't ask either out directly. Unless it's obvious to me that she's interested, I really don't want to take the risk.

Weirdly, though, Mariah stands up from her desk and walks over to my office with that feminine sway of her hips. She's wearing a red skirt that goes four inches above her smooth-as-silk knees and a short-sleeved brown button-up blouse. Her wavy, honey hair swoops around her long neck, whisps just past her shoulders, frames her angular face and those piercing hazel eyes, further framed by brown eyeliner and long, dark brown eyelashes.

When she places her hands on my desk and leans over, I gulp—her ample cleavage jiggles a bit, the white skin meeting my eyes as if inviting me in. I have to scoot forward in my chair to hide my lap from her view, since my cock is twitching and growing, making an obvious tent in my pants.

"I know you like to watch me while I work," she says in a husky voice. I see that there's a mischievous gleam in her eyes, and that mischief shows clearly through her cocky grin. "When are you going to ask me out?"

I stare at her for a moment, speechless. The universe must have favored me today! I say to Mariah, "Ms. Chase, I just didn't want to seem unprofessional."

"Don't you have balls, Boss?"

I open my mouth but forget what I was going to say. My dick won't get any softer. I guess I might as well take this opportunity to ... "Of course I do. Close the door and I'll show you."

A red blush begins to coat her face, and she bites at her lower lip. Slowly, she turns around and shuts the office door. She says as she does this, "are you really going to show me?"

My heart races. Mariah has never come onto me this blatantly, and now all I can think about is kissing those glossy pink lips and those sweet-looking breasts. "Come behind my desk, so no one can see you."

She nods her head and comes around behind me. I scoot away so she can hide under the desk, and before she does, she quickly scans the room visible through the glass door. It doesn't seem like anyone is paying us any attention, so we're safe to carry on with whatever this is turning into.

As she gets onto her knees, already breathing faster and harder, I nudge her a little with my foot so she's in the space where my legs usually go. She sits on her butt now and looks up at me with a sort of horny submissiveness that I've only encountered in porn, never in real life. I have to grab my own lap to hide the excited shakiness of my fingers.

"Show me, Boss," she whispers, unbuttoning her blouse while maintaining eye contact with me. I know the boredom of the workplace well, and it can compel people to do some wild things. Sex play with your boss really isn't that unusual under the right circumstances. There's already a power dynamic present, without any need for roleplay.

"I want to see those nipples first." I reach forward and slip my hands under her shirt before she's finished taking it off, and she lets out a cute moan when I run my hands over her nipples. I can see them now, and they're a dark red color, very perky. For some reason, my mind goes to Natalie. What would hers look like?

God. In my mind, I shake my head. Come on, there's no reason to be thinking of my father's fiancé right now when I have this sexy lady on the floor in front of me. I keep playing with Mariah's nipples and squeezing her firm breasts. Her face is all pink now, and her lip looks sore from all the biting she's been doing.

"Boss," she moans out lightly, "quit teasing me. You're so hard already." She eyes the tent in my pants. "Let me help you with that."

I shiver when she unzips my pants, and my breath hitches when she reaches her ladylike hands into my boxers and pulls my cock out. Her hot breath hits the head as she slowly begins to pump me. Next thing I know, one of her hands is cupping my balls. I fidget a bit on the chair, wanting to maintain a dominant role since that's what she seemed to be turned on by. "What are you waiting for?" I ask her, hoping this situation won't come back to bite me later. "Use your mouth."

She nods eagerly, almost like a kid who's trying to please Santa Claus by promising to be good. Then, my breath hitches when her warm lips cup the head of my penis. I'm uncircumcised, but I've always kept up with personal hygiene. Hopefully she'll find this as pleasurable for her as it is for me.

As she starts sucking, taking me in deeper and deeper with each bob of her head, I dig my fingers through her hair and give her a gentle but firm tugging. She moans, and the vibrations of her voice only add to the amazing feeling on my penis. I want to pleasure her too, so I scoot my foot in between her legs and press where her pussy is. She whines a little, ecstasy making her grind herself against my polished shoe. I have to keep myself from using her mouth as a fleshlight, and it's so damn hard not to moan loudly as she's sucking and sucking and...God, her tongue runs over the sensitive head of my cock. Oh, fuck. I can feel how wet she is through her panties and I *want to take them off so fucking badly.*

Suddenly there's a knock on the door. I scoot closer to the desk and instead of stopping, her mouth engulfs my member and I have to hold in a moan. She keeps going, albeit quieter, when Tonya opens the door and steps up to the desk. She wears an unbuttoned suit jacket over a blue blouse, and a pencil skirt. She smiles at me and flutters her black eyes, wearing her hair in an Afro today. She says, "Mr. Whitmer, I was wondering if I could take a few days off to see my brother and his kids down in Los Angeles."

"Of course," I say. I'm unable to hold back a gasp when Mariah's pace picks up and goes steady ... woah ... she's good at this.

"Are you okay, Mr. Whitmer?" Tonya asks, a look of concern falling over her beautiful brown face. She observes me, eyebrows raised.

I nod, then say, "of course."

"Okay?" She backs away slowly, taking a pen out from her jacket as she does. I try hard to keep my eyes on her face, because those knockers are ... well, I would be game if she gave me the go. "It'll be, uh, five days of vacation. I'll send you an email and mark it down on the schedule." With that, she leaves.

As soon as the door closes, I scoot back again and buck my hips into Mariah's mouth, taking control. She's drooling all over me, and her seductive eyes look up at me, as if she's asking for more.

"Fuck it." I get on the floor with her after kicking the chair back by the window, and I kiss her, fondling her breasts. Pretty soon, I'm on top of her and she's got her legs up—hooked around my hips as I use my arms to hold myself over her. I'm inside her in no time and it feels way better than her mouth. "Oh my God, Mariah ... you're a ..."

"Say it," she moans when our mouths part from a kiss.

"You're a little slut."

At that, she digs her nails across my back and bites my lip. "I'm close. Keep going," she says.

I listen, thrusting at the same pace, maybe a little harder than before. I reach down with one hand — her skirt's up around her waist — and I feel her hand as she rubs her clit. I follow that motion until she moves her hand away and begins to touch her nipples, pinching them, tugging them. I rub her clit and pound her pussy, quietly calling her a slut, while she calls me "Boss," and begs me to keep going. I'm edging inside of her, and I stare at her breasts as she plays with herself.

She's so hot but I'm not thinking much of *her* whenever my eyes drift from her face. I hate that my mind drifts to that gold digger; her attractive figure and what she might feel like ...

"I'm cumming—" Mariah's legs shake as her pussy grips my cock while it's deep inside of her. I see white when it begins to pulse, and I have to sit back and pull out, cum filling up my cupped hands.

She sits up too, panting, sweat coating her brow. "Boss," she whispers through a giggle, "you don't need to pull out next time."

My ears stop ringing. Did I hear her right the first time? "Did you just say that I should cum in you?"

She starts to button up her shirt. "No, no ..." I watch her put herself back together, and I figure it's time to follow suit. She says, "I'm only joking. You're not ready to be a father, are you?"

"Of course not!" I stare at her. I don't have enough tissues in my office to take care of the sticky mess on my hands. Anyway, I think she's being honest. Eh, I'm making myself think that. She's too hot and I've already made plans to take her with me on vacation. I guess I shouldn't assume she's crazy. One of those women who just fucks a man to get her pregnant and either marry or seek child support.

"I meant to ask earlier," I say quietly. "Would you go on a trip with me to the beach? I need a date. It's only three nights."

Mariah wraps her arms around my neck and kisses me. Then, she looks me in the eyes with her smokey gaze and says, "Of course, I'll go. That sounds exciting. Me and my boss, together for three nights. Let me know when you're going to pick me up. I'll pack tonight."

I feel relaxed knowing that I'll have someone at my side on this trip. After all, if I have Mariah with me, I won't have to think about Natalie and I'll be able to distract myself from her deceit and sex appeal. What better way is there to get along with my father's fiancé? Ignoring her on our trip is the way to go.

Chapter 4: Reflection At The Wheel

The drive southward to the condo is a beautiful one when you take the scenic route. Palm trees spring up on the grass beside the road, casting limited shade over the cars speeding below. I go slightly over the speed limit for the majority of the drive. Mariah asks if we can listen to the radio and I say, "go ahead. Feel free to change the station."

I had it on classic rock. She changes it to a station that just plays what's mainstream—for the most part it isn't bad. I find myself tapping along a bit to the upbeat rhythms and 21st century synthesizer.

When I look at her, I see that she's on her phone, scrolling through image after image of mansions and designer clothes, jewelry...

I hope she gets off her phone when we arrive at our destination. I thought she would be more talkative, since she was so upfront with me the other day. I guess she wasn't talking much when we were fucking in my office, but she seemed engaged back then at the very least.

Now, she seems perfectly content to be a passenger in my car, listening to music about sex and wealth while liking photos of riches on display. Should I say something? I have to think about *what*.

From my past interactions with Mariah, I got the impression that she wasn't particularly down to earth.

She superficially prescribed to Christianity — I had overheard her talking to a friend at work and saying how she didn't even believe Jesus was a real person. She wore a cross necklace though, perhaps to trick people into thinking she was virtuous in the ways that religious women tend to be. I don't mind anyone's personal belief in God, but as attracted as I am to Mariah, it's the facade of belief that I'm turned off by.

So, I probably shouldn't talk about religion with her. If I mention what I heard her say, she might get defensive and I'll have to drive her back home, maybe start searching for a new job. I think back on another event from work.

It happened a couple years ago. She brought a little dog into work with her and I told her she had to take it home. She shook her head and said she was just watching it for a friend and that it wouldn't be in the building for long. I warned her about our company policy against pets. She called me heartless and went to her cubicle with the small thing tucked under one arm.

Later that same day, she came to my office without the dog. I had asked her if she gave it back to her friend, and she said yes, and she was upset that I embarrassed her in front of her coworkers. I brushed that off and told her to get back to work.

Okay. I guess reflecting on our past isn't a great way to head into the future, if there is one. I'm attracted to Mariah, and I get along with her well enough at work with a few exceptions, so I shouldn't overthink this voiceless car ride. I ought to just get us the hell to the beach so Dad won't be disappointed.

Chapter 5: Day Drinking

We arrive at the condo. I get that awesome smell of ocean air breezing into the car, before I roll up all the windows. The sun is shining gloriously; there are no clouds in the sky, and I have to admit that Dad picked the best spot for the three of us to get on friendlier terms.

The registration building sits beside a huge line of white condominiums built up along a bright, clean beach. Me and Mariah get out of my car, and I go check in under the name Whitmer. I get the key and condo address, and go back outside to take Mariah to where we'll be staying for the weekend.

On this calm side road, I drive until I get to the right address, and I see that our driveway is split with Dad's condo. He texted me earlier that we would be staying right next to each other. I park next to his car and go to retrieve all of our bags.

Maria smiles at me as I do this. She's got her crocodile skin purse tucked under her arm. "Thanks for carrying the heavy stuff," she says.

I wink at her, tossing her the key. She catches it and looks confused for a moment.

"Why don't you go unlock the front door?" I ask. These condos are narrow, three floors each. I would have to walk our belongings upstairs to the master bedroom, so I figured she could do a little work.

"Oh, sure." She does this as I manage to lock the car with my less-than-free hand. We enter the house and I get our bags upstairs while she checks out the first floor. There's a nice living room with a big TV, from what I recall of how these places are set up. There's a smaller TV in the master bedroom on the third floor. The second floor, from what I saw at a glance, has a smaller bedroom and the master bath, the latter of which features a jacuzzi that I know *I'll* be using tonight.

Once I set the bags down, I take my phone out from my pocket and text Dad that I'm here with Mariah. I kick off my shoes and lie on the bed as I wait for a response. The whole place smells like lemon all-purpose cleaner. These silky sheets have that freshly washed scent that all people want from their clean laundry. To my left, there's a sliding glass door that opens up to a balcony overlooking all the sand and water. There's a small hill separating the condos from the beach, probably for privacy's sake. On that hill is a wooden pavilion with a few benches and two permanent telescopes built into the floor of it. They're not lit now, but I can make out fairy lights on the beams, wrapped around a tarp positioned to cast shade over the benches.

My phone pings. I look at it and see that it's Dad. I read his message and take a calming breath. He wants me to go down to the Tiki bar for drinks. I reply that I'll be down soon.

The Tiki bar is located a short walk away from here, also overlooking the beach like the pavilion. I already know that I want to drink light this evening, since Natalie has been occupying such a chunk of my mind lately. I don't want to do or say anything embarrassing, either embarrassing her or myself.

As I go to leave the bedroom, Mariah appears in the doorway. I don't have much time to register her before she grabs my face and pulls it toward her. Her lips press hard against mine and that's all it takes for the awkwardness of the silent ride down to dissipate into thin air.

We make out for a long time. Then, after my tongue has been inside her mouth and my hands on her now naked breasts, I throw her onto the bed and climb over her.

"Fuck me, Boss," she mewls, clawing at my back. I take my shirt off to make it easier for her, and so she can look at my six-pack. She runs her hands along my muscles, making my dick stick out, rock solid. I quickly take my pants off and she removes her skirt and wet panties.

More kissing, more fondling, and after I lift her legs up, knees over my shoulders, I push all the way inside her. She cries out in pleasure, hips angling up so I can get an even better entrance. Her arms wrap around my neck and she begs for more. "I love fucking you, baby," I moan out, thrusting slowly until she asks me to go faster, harder, deeper.

The warm, tingling waves build in intensity. I close my eyes and just listen to her music. I feel like a man: making a woman sound so animalistic, so primal. "Stay inside me," she desperately begs, wrapping her legs around my waist.

I try to pull out, but she's strong and when her pussy clamps on my throbbing cock, I can't take it anymore and I fill her up. She orgasms—I feel the muscles of her walls pulse with her heartbeat. I remove myself from her and collapse onto my side, seeing white, nearly passing out. She grabs tissues off the bedside table and helps clean me off before cleaning herself up too.

"That was amazing," she tells me through a big grin. "Best sex I've ever had."

"Better than office sex?" I asked, pleased with myself.

A coy look came over her sharp, sexy face. "*Well*, there was *one other time* ..." She gives me a light slap on the arm, laughing. "I'm joking."

"I hope so," I chuckle. After my dizziness passes, I sit up and go to rinse my dick off in the bathroom sink, since I don't want to smell like Mariah when I go see my dad and Natalie. I get out; Mariah uses the bathroom, then we walk across the sandy boardwalk to the Tiki bar.

As soon as we get to the BBQ-smelling Tiki bar, which is bustling at this hour with couples or rich families eating lunch, I spot Natalie sitting beside my dad at a table for four. She's as beautiful as the day I first met her, though she seems to be using a suntanning lotion to turn a lovely shade of honey. Her light hair hangs free to blow in the wind, pushed back only by a white headband. She wears a blue bralette under a sheer, white, loose shirt. Behind a pair of simple brown sunglasses, her big blue eyes twinkle at my dad. She's pushed her chair up against his, giving them physical contact that they otherwise wouldn't have had. He's dressed as he usually is, though he has a sunhat on his head. He's smiling at Natalie with love that I never saw him express toward my mother.

"Glad you two could make it," Dad says, standing up to shake Mariah's hand. There's a brief introduction. I tell them that Mariah's my coworker. Mariah gives me a funny look, like she doesn't quite accept my description of her.

"Sorry," I say as we sit down at the table, facing my dad and his fiancé. "Did I do something wrong?"

"No," Mariah assures me with a shake of her head. Maybe I'm wrong, but my intuition is telling me that I should be wary of her throughout our stay. She's acting closer to me than what makes sense in my mind.

Right after the waiter brings two more menus and asks what we would like to drink, he leaves, and Natalie looks at me with a strange hopefulness in her eyes. Why would she smile at me after our last interaction?

"I'm glad you could make it," she says, speaking clearly over the chatter of the other patrons. "I think we got off on the wrong foot. I'm really not a bad person —"

"You don't have to tell him that," Dad interrupts her, and granted he's not trying to be rude. She gives him a worried look and he wraps an arm around her shoulders, giving her a side-hug. "Look," he says, speaking in a casual manner that would suggest he feels no anger toward me, "Natalie is a sweet woman and she is not using me. I *want* to help her fulfill her dreams. She's working on starting up a charity that will use donation money to build housing for the homeless. It'll start in California, then spread out from here across the United States."

He kisses Natalie's temple. She melts into his side, serenity plain as day. My dad has *her* under a spell! And here I was, thinking that she must be some sort of witch.

Mariah says, with her critical eyes flickering between Dad and Natalie, "Natalie, you sound great. But can your charity really be built off of Mr. Whitmer's fortune?"

I raise my eyebrows at Mariah. "What makes you think my dad wouldn't be able to afford it?"

Dad pauses before answering her. "I can afford the initial costs, from organizing it to advertising. I have the means, and I know businessmen who would love to back Natalie's charity — as a write-off on their taxes." He then looks at me when he says, "Whitmer Real Estate is no different. The company would benefit from sponsoring this charity. It could be a big PR move." He crosses his arms and leans back in his chair. "Just think about it, Marlon. That's all I ask."

The waiter brings us our drinks. I see that Natalie has ordered a piña colada. Mariah drinks red wine, and my dad and I go for a beer.

"We're all alcoholics here," I joke. Natalie and Dad laugh. Mariah rolls her eyes and drinks.

We give the waiter our orders for lunch. I ask for shrimp linguini. Natalie and Mariah both order salads, while dad gets a cod dish. As we wait for our dishes to arrive, we get to drinking. I catch Mariah sneaking a glance at Natalie after every four or five sips.

I set my hand on her thigh under the table, giving it a squeeze. She looks at me with wide eyes and leans over to whisper into my ear, "sit closer to me, Marlon."

It wasn't often that she referred to me by my first name, but I felt like she was right to do it now. It would be a little weird for her to call me Boss in front of my dad.

"All right," I say. I scoot the chair right beside hers and keep my hand on her bare inner thigh. Even though I had intended to draw her attention away from Natalie, whenever I look directly across at the younger woman, I feel Mariah's eyes burn into the side of my head.

My dad is trying to pay Mariah no attention, probably for Natalie's sake, but he's too smart not to notice the unfriendliness she's giving off.

"What would you like to do after this?" I ask everyone.

Natalie smiles at me. "Frank and I are going to go sunbathe by the water. I got a new bikini." Her cheeks turn a shade of pink, and

I can't help but blush in response. I try to hide my own burning face in my drink, while Natalie continues with, "Sorry, I must sound like a teenager. My friends all say I'm 'too enthusiastic.'"

"That's silly to tell someone, isn't it?" Frank asks, giving Natalie a kiss on the cheek. He laughs out loud. "Anyone who's against a little enthusiasm ought to learn from you."

"I don't know ..." Mariah looks off toward one of the TV screens broadcasting sports by the bar area. "People who say that are usually realistic. They don't like exaggeration."

"True," Natalie replies, not seeming thrown off by the insinuation that she's exaggerating or unrealistic. Still, I take my hand from Mariah's leg. I don't like unwarranted criticism. "My friends are all realists. That's why they like me — I remind them to dream."

Mariah laughs, but not in a humored way like my dad did a moment ago. "Sure," she says, "that's probably why they like you."

Dad sets his drink down. I cling to mine as if it will save me from whatever the hell is going on here. Why is Mariah acting like this? If I was an idiot, I might discount the idea that she's jealous of Natalie. But I'm not. She must wish she was in Natalie's place, the lover of a man wealthy beyond her dreams, a man who's retired, and funny and kind when he wants to be.

Meanwhile, I'm not interested in making Mariah my girlfriend, not to mention a bride. After this trip I'm going to see if Tonya's available for a night out. I'll go slow with her. When I think about it, Tonya isn't exactly as beautiful as Natalie, but if I was just in it for the beauty, I wouldn't have any hope at a long-term relationship. I don't know if my life as a wealthy single man who gets some ass on the side is sustainable. Dad certainly doesn't think so.

Our food arrives and we eat. I talk to Mariah about work, wanting to distance the conversation as far as possible from Natalie's friends and enthusiasm. Sexy as Mariah is, I would be lying to myself if I claim to think that her heart is as appealing.

After we eat, Mariah says, "Marlon, let's go check out our Jacuzzi."

"You don't want to go out with us?" Dad asks, though I think he's only being polite. "We'll miss you."

"We can see you later, at dinner," I suggest. Natalie looks excitedly at me, and I can't help but chuckle.

"What?" Natalie asks, face red. Dad pulls her in for another side hug.

"That enthusiasm of yours is *very* obvious," I say. Mariah grabs my hand, silently demanding that we go. "I'm glad to see it. All right. See you later."

I go up to our waiter and pay for our meal. I also buy two bottles of fruity wine. Hopefully, that will take my mind off everything, from work to family. My romantic life is also on my mind, and I can't say it's looking great at the moment.

Mariah's already walking away when I finally leave the Tiki bar. I run up to her on the boardwalk. I feel a light sweat on the back of my neck.

It's from the sun, not nerves. A man doesn't break into a sweat just because his sexy guest is acting rude toward his dad's hotter and more likable, too-young fiancé.

"It was taking you too long," she says in a quipped manner, pursing her ruby lips at me. I keep up with her pace, and lift up the two shining wine bottles in response to her statement. Her sharp eyes flash at the bottles before returning to the wood-paneled pathway we're on. "That's nice," she says flatly. "One bottle for each of us?"

"No." I chuckle. "At least, I thought we might make them last the trip. But if you want a whole bottle, I don't get to decide that. It's your body."

"You made that clear enough back there."

I squint at her. She gets ahead of me by a foot. We keep talking, though, able to hear each other since the wind isn't strong. "Sorry, but what are you talking about?"

She says nothing. Her gaze is locked ahead.

"What's the matter?" I ask. Her lack of a response is concerning. Well, it doesn't bode well for tonight, or the rest of this trip.

A minute passes. I let out a relieved breath when she starts to speak again. Problem is, she asks, "What do you think? You're acting like you *didn't* invite me out here."

"Beg your pardon?"

She walks faster. My eyes drift to her swaying hips as I fall behind. She says loudly, "I shouldn't have to explain it."

"I don't understand what I did wrong! You're the one who was glaring at my father's fiancé!" Soon, we arrive at our condo and head inside. She hurries upstairs while I set the wine in the living room on the first floor. When I pass the second floor with the master bath, I jump a bit.

Mariah has the Jacuzzi going. She's submerged up to her shoulders in bubbling water, dark brown hair and face dripping. She must have dunked her head at some point.

"What are you staring at?" She asks me, draping her arms up on the rim of the white tub. That Jacuzzi in the corner of the room is surrounded on two sides by mirrors, so when Mariah sits up more, I'm met with at least four different angles of her naked breasts, not counting the view of them as I look straight at her.

"You're goddamn beautiful." I can't help myself!

"Yeah?" Her mouth smiles, but her eyes don't. She stands up and places her hands on her dripping wet hips. I feel aroused at the sight of her. Even so, her words don't let me give into my human impulse to fornicate. "Well, when you were looking at Natalie like a baby boy seeing tits for the first time, I got the impression you thought less of *me.*"

I cross my arms and look off toward the sink for a moment. I can see myself in the mirror there, my brown hair and lighter eyes, my tall stature — Mariah is attracted to me for a reason. I'm a handsome man.

But maybe her good-looking boss, sitting day after day in his office at a boring real-estate agency, is lacking in something that isn't looks.

I like to think I'm a competent business man, but women — it's obvious — aren't *business*. They think and feel. Being sexually or romantically involved with a woman is not "purely professional," like I was thinking it might be. No. These interactions are raw, driven by lust and desires. And I haven't been respecting that part of dating.

I brought Mariah out here with sex in mind, with distracting myself from my concerns as the main goal. Mariah must have thought about my invitation differently. Maybe she had more heart going into this than I did?

Frowning, I turn to Mariah and drop my arms at my sides. By now, the room is steaming up from the hot water in the Jacuzzi. "I'm sorry if I haven't been the best host," I say, then let out a sigh. She doesn't seem impressed by my apology.

"Whatever," she sighs too. "Are you going to join me in here, or am I standing here naked for nothing?"

My face burns and I have to look away. "Sure. I'll join you."

I unbutton my shirt. She watches me as I do. Her eyes hone in on my ripped abdomen. Just as I'm taking my pants off, she says, "I want this to last, Boss."

"I thought you were calling me Marlon now."

She huffs. Her arms cross, and she pushes her breasts up in doing so, a devious smirk crossing her lips. "I'm in a 'Boss' mood. Is that a problem, *Boss*?"

Naked, I go and enter the Jacuzzi. We sit down side by side and I wrap an arm around her shoulders. She leans her head back against my muscular bicep, her long dark hair floating around her head when she goes neck-deep in the water. The Jacuzzi jets feel amazing on my back, and I tilt my head back and close my eyes. My breath steadies and my heart rate slows as I melt into the peace of this moment.

I wonder what Natalie is doing at this moment. If I was out on the beach with her and Dad, I would likely see her in her bikini. Whether my dad funds Natalie's career or not, I have to know if it's love. He's old, she's young. I might have been wrong thinking that she's manipulating him. Even so, I *have* to know if she loves him or not. I won't feel at ease until I can be sure without a single doubt.

Mariah's delicate hand traces down my chest, finding its way to my pelvis. Then, she takes a hold of my dick and starts playing with it. "Do you like that, Boss?" she whispers huskily into my ear. I nod, grinning as my dick hardens in her grasp.

"Of course. Keep going, Ms. Chase." I reach down between her legs under the water and slowly run my hand over her hot, swollen clit. Her breath hitches, and I tuck my face in her neck, kissing her, making her moan. "If you play nice," I growl in her ear, and feel her shutter beneath me, "I'll give you a promotion."

"Oh, Boss." Her hand keeps pumping as I keep rubbing her pussy. I slip two fingers inside. I want to take her, but for now I'll make her shiver under my touch.

"You're being *very good*, Ms. Chase." I lean over her and kiss her soft, strawberry-tasting lips. She gasps when I reach deep inside of her and rub fast against the front-facing wall, all tender and juicy. Her eyes roll back and her mouth opens as I finger her harder and faster. She tries to close her legs but I stick my leg between them before she can, only working her more intensely.

She's moaning and her hands tremble too much to keep jerking me off. "Boss" she whimpers, "I'm gonna cum."

I command her: "You better."

Chapter 6: Opposites Don't Attract

Mariah and I are buzzed by the time the sun is setting and Dad texts me, reminding me about dinner. I get the ping when I'm lying on the bed with Mariah, who lies naked beside me, blanket by her waist. I text Dad that we'll be down in a few minutes, then I roll over and kiss Mariah's breasts. She leans into it, smiling, eyes closed. I suck on her nipples and just as she's getting more into it, I bring my lips up to hers to kiss her. Then I whisper, "Dinnertime, baby."

She sighs, disappointed. "You had me thinking you were ready for round six!" In a flash, she's out of bed and fishing for a cocktail dress from her travel bag.

I briefly stare at her shapely ass, before getting up to search my suitcase for something nice. All of my clothes are casual, but still fit for work and dinner. I throw on a button-up blue, short-sleeved shirt that adds to my triangular build — that's broad shoulders and a slim waist. I put on some white slacks and brown sandals, a gold watch, and I run a brush through my light brown hair and beard. When I glance at myself in the bathroom mirror, brushing my teeth just to freshen up, I feel a sense of confidence that isn't always there. Having sex with Mariah must be increasing my testosterone, because I feel like a *man*. Like *the man*.

"You ready to go?" I ask, stepping out from the bathroom. Mariah's wearing a dark red dress, looking fantastic at every curve. She's redone her makeup since it got messy earlier, and has her hair brushed, straight and free.

"Ready," she says with a laugh. "Are you impressed by my speed?"

"Absolutely. I don't know how you got ready so fast — faster than me, that's for sure."

We leave the condo and head over to meet Frank and Natalie at the Tiki bar. Since it's darker outside, the fairy lights are on and light the place aglow from a distance.

"So pretty," Mariah muses beside me. Without warning, she smacks my ass. I jump a little, and she smirks, eyes piercing me like a hook through a fish's mouth.

I don't know what to say, so I walk a little slower to put her ahead of me a few inches.

"Aren't you going to punish me, Boss?" she asks a little too loudly. Even though there aren't many people walking around on the boardwalk at the moment, the thought of our sexuality being put on display without the pro of physical pleasure makes me both nervous and irritable.

"Later, Mariah," I say. She huffs. I guess that's not the answer she wanted.

Once we enter the Tiki bar, we're handed dinner menus and directed to Dad's table, which this time directly faces the ocean on the far end of the open patio. Glass fires burn low where flower boxes might have gone around the perimeter. The smell of smoked shellfish and chowder fills the air, making me salivate.

And Natalie? I can't take my eyes off of her. She sits next to my dad, wearing a flowy green dress shimmering against the fairy lights and the fire's glow. She's a mermaid surrounded by land-legged men and women, ethereal in appearance and in how she motions her arms at my dad, brushing some of his leftover hair behind his ear.

"Come on, Marlon." Mariah grabs my hand and tugs me toward the table. It takes me a moment to snap back to reality. We all greet each other, and me and Mariah sit across from them like we had earlier. This time, Mariah is directly across from my dad, and I have the perfect view of Natalie, who sets a tanned elbow on the table as she rests her chin on the palm of her hand.

"You look like you got sun," I comment, reaching for the glass of water Dad has given me — he has politely ordered all of us a glass before we arrived. The warm air is fluctuated with the cool sea breeze, so the ice in the water wasn't entirely necessary. I appreciate it, though.

"I did," Natalie says, smiling at me. "Frank and I spent the whole day outside. You should join us tomorrow! It'll be fun."

"I don't think we will," Mariah snaps. She wears a fake look of pleasantry, which any man and his dog could see through. "Marlon and I are going yachting."

"Are we?" I cross my arms and squint at Mariah. She raises her eyebrows at me, as if I had said something rude.

"Yachting?" Natalie leans forward, giving Mariah a closer look without losing the sparkle in her widened eyes. "That sounds cool. Doesn't it, Frank?"

Frank nods at Natalie, then goes back to raising an eyebrow at my date. "I've been. It's a party out on the water."

"Could we go with you, Mariah?" Natalie asks, seeming eager. I wish I could get a better read on this woman. I can't tell if she's just a turn-the-other-cheek chick or if she didn't catch the rudeness in Mariah's response to her earlier.

I feel a light sweat forming on the back of my neck as I observe the women and my silent but agitated father.

A saccharine smile appears on Mariah's angular face. When she talks, it's as if she's speaking to a child. "Oh, no, it's a lot to handle. All the alcohol and half-naked men." She side-eyes me. It takes me a moment to realize that it's me she's about to address, in front of my dad and Natalie. "For a woman in a *committed* relationship, it'll ruin whatever you have going on with the hubby, but for me? It's heaven on Earth."

"You can go, then," I say sharply.

Mariah raises her eyebrows at me, blinking.

Dad says, "Cut it out, you two. You're making a scene."

"No, I want to hear your son," Mariah snaps back at my dad. Natalie looks shaken, and her lips are sealed shut as she too watches in horror at whatever the hell is about to take place.

I sigh, shaking my head. "Mariah, we *just* started seeing each other. If you want an open relationship, I don't care. Go ahead. But don't expect me to chase after you like a little boy."

At first, I think only silence will follow. But Mariah quickly subverts my assumption.

"Says the man who invited me here!"

My dad shushes Mariah when the waiter comes over and takes our drink orders. Natalie is giving me a perturbed look, but I don't know why. What did *I* do wrong here? I wish I could grab her by those delicate shoulders and give her a light shake and say, *can't you see? My date is out to get you!* But what good would that do? As the man in this situation, I'm obligated to defend the woman I'm with. However, seeing as Mariah wants to chastise me in front of my dad and is trying to make a fool of me to these two, I would rather call her out on her bullshit than pretend like I've done something horribly offensive.

"Let's enjoy our dinner," Dad says forcefully. Natalie puts a comforting arm around his old shoulders and gives him a kiss on the cheek. "Thanks, baby girl," he tells her.

Even though I shouldn't laugh at the phrase, I do. He and Natalie give me a confused look.

"It's just that you called her 'baby girl,'" I explain, unable to keep a humored grin off my lips. "And with your age difference, that's what she might as well be."

Natalie giggles, to my surprise. Dad's eyes go wide at her — he must be surprised too. His tanned fiancé gives him a hug, then says, looking at me, "I'll give you that, Marlon."

My heart flutters. I have to cross my arms and lean back in my chair, pressing my lips together. Her response seems genuine. Obviously, she's able to laugh at herself, a skill most people I've encountered lack.

She continues with, "If I wasn't with Frank, I think the waiter might have handed me a kid's menu."

Frank and I laugh. Mariah seethes to my right.

The waiter brings us our drinks, and we order meals. I get a grilled salmon dish, which Natalie also orders. Mariah says, "Just a Caesar salad," and I'm pretty sure she's denying herself a better meal to spite me — I expect her to make a claim later that I put her in a bad mood and therefore she's hungry because of me, and I should treat her to something expensive or whatever.

Dad gets a sirloin steak. He and Natalie start talking about a trip they're planning for next winter, to the Alps. They want to go skiing, and I let Dad know that he's crazy if he thinks skiing at his age is a good idea. Meanwhile, I feel Mariah's hand trace along my thigh with a harsher touch than usual. Does she want me horny, or hurt? Both, maybe.

We eat, dinner ends, and I think I know why Mariah and Natalie are so weird together: they're opposites. While Natalie has a sense of humor, Mariah won't laugh at herself — only at other people.

I guess it's not the worst thing in the world, this age-gap relationship Dad and Natalie have going on. Maybe Natalie's advantaged by Dad's money, but Dad is obviously in love with her, and she clearly loves him.

Seeing how Mariah is acting toward me tonight, whether it's out of jealousy of Natalie's situation and personality or her belief that I want to fuck Natalie instead of her, I know that I need a Natalie in my life. Frankly, I would rather have a generous sugar baby over a selfish one like Mariah, if that's what they are.

I don't have to worry about Natalie and dad. Really, I need to worry about myself. Mariah looks about ready to kill me as we walk back to our condo. When we enter it and shut the door behind us, she turns to me and demands in a biting voice, "fuck me, Marlon."

"Where's this coming from?"

She grabs my hands and makes me touch her breasts. I don't react.

"Feel me," she says, glaring at me. "You've been ignoring me all day!"

"How have I been ignoring you?" I pull my arms away from her breasts and head upstairs to the bathroom. She grabs the back of my shirt while I'm climbing the steps and I have to stop in my tracks, so she can't yank me down. "What the hell do you think you're doing? This isn't appropriate."

"Appropriate?" She gives me a shocked expression. "I'm on a romantic trip with my boss, and you're saying now that *I'm acting inappropriately.*"

"Fine," I concede, looking down at the steps. "I made a mistake. I shouldn't have invited you here. That was a bad move on my part, and I'm sorry."

She wipes at her eyes, leaving a trail of runny mascara on her cheeks. When did she start crying? "Sorry doesn't make it right," she cries quietly. "I like you, Marlon. But it's obvious you don't like me."

Guilt nibbles at me, but even though I touch her shoulder to comfort her, I stand my ground in message. "And for that reason, Mariah, I think it's best that I call you a cab first thing tomorrow and get you home. It's not *you*, it's me."

Mariah shrugs my arm off and hurries upstairs past me. I don't follow her. Instead, I use the restroom and go to the first floor right after, where I lay on the couch. I'll sleep here tonight to give her space, and I'll go back upstairs tomorrow morning to check on her. That's the right thing to do.

Chapter 7: Early Morning Exhibition

Early the next morning, I go upstairs to check on Mariah. My back aches from sleeping on the couch, but I'm glad to have gotten at least some sleep. After I open the bedroom door, I see her asleep beneath the bedsheets of the queen-sized bed. I take the opportunity to observe her for a moment as she's sleeping. The sharp features on her face seem softer when she's unconscious, and I feel grateful for that — if I'm lucky and she fulfills her promise of calling a cab first thing when she wakes up, I'll may be spared from whatever rage must be left in her system.

I don't see a purpose in waking her up, so I walk past the bed to go outside on the balcony. I want to watch the sun, which is only now just peeking out over the horizon. Quietly, I open the sliding glass door, step out, and close it behind me. Fresh, salty ocean air hits me. I breathe in deeply as my eyes take in the sky as it transitions from a pale green shade to bright orange. When I was really young, Mom and Dad liked to compete with one another — who could show me the better sunset. I had taken a trip to Brazil when I was around nine years old, and the look of the sun on those white sandy beaches had to have been the best sight I've ever seen.

Mom took me there, back then. She won. The best sunset my dad had ever shown me was up in the mountains of Colorado. But I'm a beach man, and as a boy nothing drew me in quite like the Pacific.

I take a seat on a white, reclining beach chair. The cool air is quickly warming, but there doesn't seem to be anyone outside at this hour.

Bzzz.

What's that? Something is buzzing. It's a low, static noise. I glance to my right and my heart jumps when I spot Natalie on her balcony. Because of the angles of our condos, I can only make out half of theirs, and I suspect that Natalie can't see me. Besides, her back is turned toward me. Still, I can't break my stare.

She wears a white robe, but she has draped it over her chair, revealing a pair of bare shoulders. Is she naked? Must be.

Her head lulls back on the seat. Over the sound of crashing waves and a small vibrator, I can hear her panting. Based on the wetness of her hair, I suspect that she's just gotten out of the shower. Dad probably took her place in the bathroom, and it's obvious that she's pleasuring herself out here.

God my dick is hard. I watch her and listen to her as I unzip my pants and pull out my cock. I begin jerking off. I keep my lips sealed, because I don't want her to know that I'm here. Even if she's naked on a balcony — I suspect that she's into voyeurism given this circumstance — if she were to discover *me* masturbating to *her*, there would be trouble.

Pleasurable waves wash throughout my body as I keep at it. I never look away from the back of Natalie's head, and her increasingly fast and erratic breathing is only making me harder. It hurts, how aroused I am. I want to be inside of her, this young, beautiful woman. I want to be the one making her moan and whimper, making her toes curl, making her orgasm.

I close my eyes and picture us making love. It's nothing like how Mariah and me fuck. It's vanilla. It's joyful, it's sweet, it's intimate.

"Hngh—"

I cum suddenly. It shoots over the balcony railing. I hope no one was walking on the sidewalk below me.

I pull a tissue out from my pocket and clean myself off. Standing, I hurry inside and shower. I didn't look at Natalie after I came. I hope that my involuntary grunt didn't alert her to my presence on the adjacent balcony.

While I shower, I scrub myself thoroughly. What kind of son does that to his father's fiancé? Masturbating felt so fucking good at the time, and the picture of Natalie I held in my head was sublime. My imagination usually isn't very wild — this morning hits different.

There's a knock on the bathroom door. "What is it?" I ask loudly, so Mariah can hear me through the door and the running shower. I thank the steam that has built up in the room over my hour-long shower, because Mariah responds to my question by breaking in.

"I'm leaving," she snaps at me. I open the shower's opaque door just a crack so I can see her properly, without any distortion.

"All right," I say.

"Do you have anything you want to say before I go?"

"Let me see ... no."

"You asshole!"

I shut the shower door and go on scrubbing myself. When she doesn't leave, I bite back meaner words I can think of and demand respectfully, "Get out of the condo. Please."

She slams the door behind her. A relieved sigh escapes me, but overall, I'm not feeling great. I hang my head and let the water massage my scalp. All I can do now is pray that Mariah doesn't go to HR. Also, pray that Natalie didn't see me this morning.

Chapter 8: What Am I Thinking?

I'm sitting on my bed with my phone in my hands, eyes glued to the screen. Mariah has sent me a hefty number of texts.

Ur such a douchebag!

Why the fuk would u invite me? Ur a man child n treated me like shit

Go jump off the dock motherfucker

"Jesus Christ." Sweat is starting to drip down the back of my neck. These messages were all from after she left this morning. Without a doubt, she's still pissed out of her mind. Damn it! And she'll be back to work before me. If she makes a formal statement against me, I'll be in big trouble. It's time to do some damage control.

I text her. *I'm sorry that I treated you poorly. You agreed to go on vacation with me thinking that you were my date, and you were. But I'm not interested in you romantically and it is in our best interests that we keep our differences to ourselves and move forward with respect and dignity.*

That oughta do it. I hit send and take a deep breath. Dad taught me many years ago that the best way to handle an angry woman is to agree with her and divert the subject to something positive. Mutual respect and dignity sound positive to me. But I'm afraid it may not be enough.

I start another message. This one should ensure my safety. *In other news, I hear the weather's going to be great these next few weeks. So, I'm going ahead and giving everyone five days off next week. I'll make an official announcement shortly. Enjoy the extra vacation days. Also, bonuses are coming early this year.*

The latter was a lie, but that's why I said "this year" instead of giving a specific timeframe in which she can expect a bonus. Pretend good news is still good news.

For a few minutes, I exit out of my messages and play some online solitaire. I'm halfway done when I hear a ping — she's responded to my messages. My heart pounds as I click on her text notification, and proceed to read what she has sent me.

I appreciate the apology. Never treat me that way again and we can call it even. I would like us to keep the events of this trip private as well. I don't need you ruining my reputation.

The last part doesn't make sense. How would *I* ruin *her* reputation? Whatever. The fact that she's not going to make a fuss at work is enough for me to feel safe and secure.

A major weight has just been lifted off my shoulders. If Mariah makes no stink at work, then we can put this unfortunate trip behind us. We don't need to fight each other — she doesn't need me to date her and I don't need her to pine after me. It's about damn time that we *live and let live*, as the saying goes.

Now, if I can only be sure that Natalie didn't see me on the balcony …

*

At noon, I meet Dad and Natalie on the beach. Hot sound caresses my feet as I walk around in leather sandals. The couple have a nice setup going on, with a big blue umbrella to cast shade over them, and two reclining beach chairs that have drink holders currently holding piña coladas.

"Is the devil gone?" Dad asks, chuckling. Based on how he's dressed, he could be a tourist in Hawaii.

"She is." I say with a laugh. Then, I take a seat on one of the beach towels laid out in front of them, half in the shade and half in sunshine. "It'll be okay at work — I'm sure that's what you're worried about."

Dad nods. "Of course, I wouldn't want to be in your position. But if you say it'll be okay, I believe you, kid."

I look back at the two of them. "We talked it over, and she wants to move on too. I'm sorry for inviting her, guys. I expected her to be more fun than that."

Natalie smiles at my dad before looking at me with a pleasant expression. Part of me thinks that I'm seeing uncertainty in her eyes — I can't tell for certain, though, so I shove my anxious thoughts aside.

"Put on some sunscreen," Natalie suggests, handing me a bottle of the sun lotion.

I lather it on the parts of my skin that aren't covered by my clothes, then pass it back to her with a casual, "thanks."

We're on the beach for a while longer, then we head to the Tiki bar to have lunch. We each order something light, and Dad is tipsy from all the alcohol he's been drinking. Natalie likes to cuddle up with him. With the aid of two margaritas, I'm feeling better than earlier and it doesn't take long for my anxiety to completely disappear.

"If you excuse me, I have a date with the bathroom," Dad jokes shortly after our meals have arrived. I'm in the middle of eating shrimp linguini when he walks off toward the men's room.

It's then that the chill atmosphere at our table shifts. I'm hit with an uneasy feeling when Natalie says, "Hey, Marlon, can we talk?"

"Oh ... sure."

There's a deep frown on her beautiful face, and I'm struggling to maintain eye contact. The guilt I felt earlier is back, with a vengeance. Based on the concern darkening her eyes, she isn't feeling very different.

"I noticed you earlier."

Shit. My heart races. I gulp down air, then reach for my glass of water and chug it down.

Natalie's eyes start looking glassy. Her lip quivers for a moment, but she appears to pull herself together. She speaks quietly, obviously wanting this conversation to be as private as it can be, with it taking place in a public setting.

"It hurts me that you watched me while I ..." Her cheeks turn a bright shade of red, and her gaze falls for a second. I watch as she wrings her hands on the table, next to her salad bowl. "I didn't know you were watching until you, um ... until you came."

I stop breathing, and say nothing. My eyes grow wide. She sounds ashamed, and the blush suggests as much, yet there's something else she's feeling. I can't put my finger on it.

"As you know, I love Frank," she continues. Her shoulders are pinched up, close to her ears, and she slouches forward ever so slightly.

When her eyes meet mine, I catch a twinkle in hers. I feel bad about it, but even now, with these serious circumstances and our mutual shame, I'm aroused.

"I know you love him," I reply gently.

"I wasn't trying to wrong him. I just wanted some time to myself, to ... you know."

I nod.

"We can't do this again."

"Of course, we can't."

Her eyes flicker up at me. Defensively, she snips, "You're perverted."

I shake my head at this. "Masturbating on a balcony is kinky — *I'm* not the pervert here. Anyone could have seen you if they looked up at the right spot on the dock."

She lowers her head, lips pressed together. "Please, don't tell Frank."

"I never would tell my dad something like that. And likewise. Don't say anything. It'll kill him."

"Of course. We'll pretend like it didn't happen. I don't want Frank to feel insecure."

"Me either."

And I hate to think this even, but now that I know Natalie wants to protect my father's feelings, I only feel warmer inside. I feel warm *for her*. She's well-intentioned, and I really don't need to worry about them.

But I would be a liar if I didn't admit that *I want Natalie for myself*.

Chapter 9: A Hot Tub Encounter

"Her yacht idea wasn't bad," Dad says. Then, he nurses his orange vodka.

I've taken to sitting beside him and Natalie on a reclining foldable chair that I bought at the nearest tourist shop within walking distance. Since lunch is over, we have the rest of the day to do whatever we want. And the yachts floating out on the open water seem to be calling us.

Natalie is next to my dad, using him to block me from view, it seems. I'm sure she's still thinking about this morning. Even so, she goes along with the conversation as if nothing else is on her mind. "I would *love* to go out on the ocean. We can hitch a ride, can't we? Daddy?"

I cringe.

Dad reaches a hand over and gives her shoulder an impassioned squeeze. "Of course, baby!" He grins like a madman. *That's* a look I don't see often. "Daddy's got it covered." He glances at me and says, "We would love for you to come with us, Marlon."

While the idea of partying on a yacht seems great, I can't help but feel a little uncomfortable at their PDA. Yes, they're adults and can do whatever the hell they want, but can't Natalie call Dad something other than "Daddy" in front of me?

Maybe it's on purpose? Maybe she's trying to reignite a sexual spark between her and my father, to get over this morning's awkward encounter. *That* I can understand, but it's still gross in my book.

"Let's find the wharf," Dad says, finishing off his vodka then standing out of his chair. He starts packing his stuff. "Let's drop this off at the condo, Natalie. I don't want anything to get stolen."

"Right-o." Natalie helps pack up their belongings. I join in, folding my chair. The sun's starting to beat down on me. I guess I'll be lathering on sunscreen when I get back to the condo.

"Hey, Marlon," Dad says after we've begun to walk back, "you shouldn't mention the yachts to Mariah at work. She might get jealous."

I nod my head, agreeing completely. "She's the jealous type. I never would have expected her to act the way she did toward Natalie."

Natalie, who isn't far behind us, hurries to Dad's side and says, "Why would she be jealous of me?"

Dad has both of their chairs in his arms as she carries the bags with their towels and extraneous supplies. If he wasn't already occupied, he would probably be patting her on the back right now, trying to comfort her. "You're a wonderful girl, baby," he says with a sigh. "That might be why."

"I don't know ..." Natalie's green eyes drift toward the open waters running alongside the wooden walkway, separated only by a sandy shore.

"Don't worry, baby. You did nothing wrong."

My heart thumps when Natalie's gaze momentarily locks on mine. I look away, quickly watching where I step. I feel my dad's eyes burn into my side for a moment, but it's brief, and soon they're both just looking forward, watching where they walk.

I don't like this. Not at all.

*

The wharf is pretty busy today, and I'm glad that the stress of trying to find my dad's new friend Joe is distracting me from all the previous events of the day. As soon as I got back from the beach, I had thrown myself on the bed and buried my head for around twenty minutes. While the cool of the sheets and pillow eased chipped away at some of the tension trapped in my body, I couldn't get rid of it completely.

That's what this party yacht is supposed to do — I hope it will, anyway — it'll clear my brain and body of all remaining tension.

I walk past a group of teenage girls and boys. They're wearing minimal clothes over their swimsuits, but everything on them is designer — Gucci, Supreme, California Sky, Barton Perreira — you get the picture.

I spot Dad and Natalie speaking to a forty-something-year-old man who's got a lot of pepper in his still full head of hair. I have to squeeze between an elderly couple and a fat guy to get to them.

"Hey, fellas." I hold my hand out.

Joe shakes my hand and says, "We were just talking about you, Marlon." His accent is notably influenced by the Mexican immigrants living here in SoCal. "Frank told me you brought a scary chikita to the condo."

I begin to grimace, but force the amicable smile to return to my face. Still, I squint at my dad, trying to send the message that I don't want him telling any random-ass person about my coworker. But he shrugs, laughing off my unvoiced anger.

"Amigos, come on board!" Joe urges us onto his good-sized, recently-cleaned yacht. Nicki Minaj blasts from speakers onboard.

Soon, I find myself lost in a small crowd of young adults, many of whom I'm positive are in college. While brine is the dominant odor, I pick up on a lot of sweat and sunscreen. Oh, perfumes too. I make my way toward the stern, wanting more space and a better view of the water.

I have to avert my eyes on occasion; the sun shines so brightly against the waves. We're yet to take off, but that's no big deal. I'm glad to be out of the office, and even gladder that Mariah's gone — but don't get me wrong, I don't hate her. This trip has just proven to be worse when she's around. Besides, now I'm free to flirt with good-looking ladies. I just hope to find someone who already has a bachelors.

Looking at my selection of ladies, I adjust my sunglasses. There aren't many that seem to fit my two standards: educated and employed. It wouldn't surprise me if some of these women were paid to come hang out and hook up with men. Maybe Joe is the one who organized the whole shebang?

Hold on. A girl is walking up to me. She's wearing pink sunglasses and her short hair is dyed bleach blonde. I would bet on her being a size 0. Tall, slim, dark tan, cherry colored bikini.

"Hey, handsome," she greets me in a grating valley girl accent. "Are you, like, thirty years old?"

I freeze where I'm standing and take her in, voice included. I can't be the only person who finds the vocal fry unattractive. But she's hot, so I try to open my mind more to a possible hookup — I don't think I could date someone with an annoying voice long-term.

"Is that your business?" I ask jokingly. She gives me a wide grin and lightly slaps my chest with the back of her limp wrist.

"Wow! You're, like, ready to fight!" Another tipsy laugh. "Fine. If you don't want to tell me your age, can you, like, tell me your name?"

Amused, I say, "What? I can't hear you over the music."

This time, she's shouting. "What's your name, dude?" I can hear her just fine, but an idea has popped into my head. Gotta take it.

"You know what? I just can't hear you out here. Is there a quieter place inside?"

She nods, then takes my hand. "Okay, that's cool. Whatever. I'll show you."

I'm led through the crowd. As she pulls me along, I search for my dad and Natalie. There they are, toward the back of the boat. I would say hi if I hadn't noticed an older couple talking to them.

"In here." My surprise guide tugs me inside the body of the yacht. We're met first with bookshelves and a sofa, some chairs, and a kitchenette. Then she lifts a round door near a desk and we climb down a short ladder into some bedrooms. The walls look wooden, though the outside of the ship doesn't suggest a wooden make. I feel us bob slightly with the water, and the crowd on the floor above us makes the ceiling pop and groan.

"Will this collapse on us?" I ask, mostly joking. Then again, I don't know the structural integrity of this yacht. Now would be a bad time to find out that it's poor.

"We're fine down here. Like, I've been a million times." The tiny woman has shut the door leading into the room, and she sits on one of two unmade beds, basically planting herself on a pile of wrinkled navy sheets and a gray comforter.

"Is this your yacht?"

She curls her index finger toward herself, gesturing that I come closer. Nice. I feel a rush of excitement at the thought of us being down here, hooking up while everyone else, strangers and family alike, are oblivious upstairs.

"Just kiss me, dummy." Grabbing me by the head, she literally forces me into a kiss. However, it's only forced for half a millisecond. As soon as I realize this is an invitation to fuck, I board that ship.

"What's your name?" I ask her between deep kisses. Only a minute has passed since I climbed over her, her lying flat on her back with her legs wrapped around my waist. We're clothed still, though her covers are already minimal.

"Paris," she whispers. Her lips press together to suppress a moan — I've slipped my hand below her waist to rub on her clit through her swimsuit. My fingers are getting wet, and they're warm from all the heat that's radiating from between her legs. "Who're you?" she asks. A gasp escapes her when I massage her down there, gently rubbing and rolling on her.

"Marlon," I say.

Lowering my head to the top of her bikini, I bite the securing string for the garment. It's tied at the front, thank God.

Grunting as an animal might, I pull my head back and manage to undo the knot. Her breasts bounce slightly when the cups of the bikini fall down between her arms. She blushes as I take her B-cups in, all the while stimulating her with my hand.

"What do you think?" she asks me eagerly. Yet, there's something wrong. She isn't gasping so much, and her smile is beginning to fall.

"What do I think ... of you?" I ask. I hope I didn't do anything to upset her. If I did, I don't know what that wrong could possibly be.

"Of these," she specifies more seriously, gesturing her hands at her chest. I look into her brown eyes. Her sunglasses have fallen off onto the floor, next to mine — I don't remember taking them off, though I guess sex *is* distracting. Anyway, my erection isn't as strong as it was a moment ago. I can see a sad glimmer in her eyes. They're glassier than they should be, likely with the beginnings of tears.

Damn the world. There's no reason a woman should feel bad about herself for having breasts of *any* size. Hell! She could have no breasts and that wouldn't make her unattractive, per se. There's her ass, her hips, her silky arms and legs, and her face.

"These breasts," I reply, kissing each of her hard nipples, "are fantastic."

"Fuck — yes!" She grinds against my hand and beams as she does so, not looking at me but rather squeezing her eyes shut and tilting her head back. I smile. I guess that's what she needed to hear.

Suddenly, she reaches down for my pants. "I want you inside me," she says, unzipping me.

Once my cock is out, it only takes a few seconds for me to slip her out of her bikini completely, and for me to slip past her swollen lips to be fully inside her. She's moaning, and the walls of her vagina are making my eyes water as they squeeze me, holding me inside her.

Her elbows rest on my shoulders as her hands clasp against my back.

"You're so fucking big," she whines, biting her lower lip. "Bigger than my boyfriend."

I pause. While her tight pussy is screaming to be fucked, I'm starting to connect some dots. If she has a boyfriend, and she knows this boat and has been down in this area a million times, then she would be dating the owner of the boat. "Your boyfriend isn't an older guy named Joe, is he?"

Her eyes go big for a moment. "Um. No?"

Before my conscience can make a decision, she starts to work her hips back and forth, making me thrust in and out of her. I hold myself up with my arms as she uses me. This doesn't feel right, but my body doesn't agree with my brain and I end up doing the work.

We keep it quiet. She has more trouble doing this than I do, but she doesn't seem all that worried about alerting the partiers to our presence down the hatch. She squirts when I pound her until she orgasms, and I pull out and cum on her stomach.

The pleasure passes, my brain fog is cleared. Now, all that's left in me is guilt. Shame and guilt. I had sex with another man's woman. Most likely Joe's. I don't believe that Paris would tell me the truth had I guessed right.

"Help me clean up," she says drowsily. I follow her eyes to a roll of paper towels across from the bed, on the floor.

"All right. Sure." I go and grab the paper towels and take some for myself before handing her the rest.

"That was cool, dude," Paris says through a soft laugh. When she wipes, she wipes gingerly.

"You're welcome?"

Now is the time to leave. I climb the ladder after fixing my clothes. All I want to do now is go back to my condo and sleep the night away. Instead, when I get out of there and back onto the deck, only then does it hit me.

We're nowhere near shore. The partying is more intense, the music louder, the briny smell stronger. I walk toward the back of the boat, trying to find Dad and Natalie. As I do so, I'm hit with another wave of guilt. Natalie may not have cheated on my dad, but I knew what I was doing when I jerked off to her this morning.

I knew. And, in that sense, that means I cheated on my dad. It was wrong. Yet, like with Paris just minutes ago, I kept going and I finished. And I want to finish again, but not with Paris. Not with Mariah. Not by myself. I want to be with Natalie.

But I can't. Not if I want to consider myself a moral man.

Then again, morals don't make people millionaires.

*

The party goes late into the night. For the last five hours, I've been wandering the deck in search of booze and intellectual conversation. So far, I blew a blood alcohol content of .07 and I conversed with some younger men about the exorbitant cost of living in California. Even being situated so close to a massive fault line, it seems that the imminent threat of natural disaster doesn't do much for the buyer. While I'm not a buyer's market kind of guy, I've worked with enough average folks to feel sorry for anyone looking to buy a house in this great state of ours.

"Marlon! Hey!" Dad breaks through the crowd, walking up to me with red cheeks visible in the flashing lights of the party boat. It's otherwise dark out here and only the moon and impressive number of stars provides us with natural lighting. Anyway, Dad's hand lands on my shoulder. His other hand holds a drink with a green olive stuck on a toothpick floating around in the pale liquid. "I've been looking everywhere for you. Seems like you disappeared for the whole day."

"Disappeared?" I raise an eyebrow at him. He's slurring a little. "That's strange, because I've been around this entire time." My mind flashes to the hookup I had earlier with who I can only assume is Joe's girlfriend, and I decide to keep that experience secret. I don't want to get tossed off the boat. "What about you and Natalie? Where is she?"

"Natalie went inside to chat with a few friends from college," Dad says with a smile. "I swear, she has friends on every corner of the Earth. That woman can shake hands better than anyone I've ever met.

Hell—better than myself!" He slaps my shoulder, laughing. "She's got enemies too, but who doesn't? Mariah's one of them now, isn't that right? Your mother would've hated Natalie, too."

"I don't know, Dad. I think she would have hated *you* for being with a much younger woman."

We seem to be heading toward the shore now. Still, the music is loud and the multicolored lights are flashing down on us from the roof of the yacht. Seeing as my dad is drunk, I would like us to get back fast. Maybe he's different now that he's older, but he can be a bastard when drunk. Inconsiderate, anyway.

"Lonny, boy, your mother would hate me being with *anyone*."

"You mean like how she hated being with you?"

He glares, but that aged gaze softens and he lets out a chuckle, shaking his head. Again, he plants his hand on my shoulder. "Just like that, Lon. Exactly."

We stand still for a moment, considering each other. Then, he takes his hand off my shoulder and walks toward the door leading inside the yacht, to the room with all the books that Natalie is allegedly hanging out in.

I wonder if he knows that it was his fault. I love my dad, but he wasn't a great husband to Mom back in the day, and he certainly didn't parent me until I was in high school. Mom did the hardest work, even if she wasn't making the money.

I'm sure he treats Natalie well. She says he does. I don't know if I should tell her more about why Dad and Mom broke up, because I'm biased in favor of Natalie leaving him, even though I want him to be happy. I wish I had a brother or sister who could do the talking for me. That way, it wouldn't be me sabotaging their relationship.

God, what am I thinking? I'm seriously thinking about shit talking Dad? I must be out of my mind. He's not a bad guy — he really isn't. Maybe it's moral to let them work things out on their own, but acting moral won't guarantee my happiness.

I'll keep thinking about it.

*

"Thanks for helping me get Frank into bed," Natalie says quietly, smiling in an apologetic manner that suggests that she's embarrassed by Dad's drunkenness. We had to walk him back after we disembarked. He's asleep in their king-sized bed, on his side. Natalie vanishes for a couple seconds and comes back with a small trash bin with a little plastic bag inside. She sets it beside the bed, within Dad's reach. "In case he pukes," she says when she turns back toward me.

I give a slight smile. She looks like she's had a long day, hair a bit of a mess and makeup a little runny, probably from the heat and ocean spray.

"Are you tired?" she asks, placing her hands on her hips.

"Well, to be honest, I would like to use that hot tub by the swimming pool."

I had only used the condo's indoor Jacuzzi with Mariah. There's a pool and hot tub outside, located near our two condos. We can access it with a second key on the condo key ring. Neither pool nor hot tub are large, since they're meant to be shared by the four condos located closest to it. We had walked past it while helping Dad home, and it was empty, lit up by blue underwater lights.

"You do?" Natalie's eyes glitter. With a touch of excitement in her voice, she says, "okay, this might sound crazy, but I was thinking about taking a swim. In the hot tub, not the pool — that's too cold at night."

She still has her swimsuit on. I can make it out through her loose clothes. My lower half is feeling very warm suddenly. "I don't know," I say, "I might just hit the hay."

A frown appears on her doll-like lips. "No. Give me company. Please."

"It's ... it's late."

I start to turn my back toward her to head on out, but she reaches for me and takes my wrist. I shiver with excitement. If she's not careful, I might forget that my dad exists.

When I look at her expression, it seems that she wasn't expecting her own response to my leaving. She lets go of me and steps back, letting out a cute, nervous cough. Then she whispers, eyes looking off to the side as a blush spreads across her cheeks. "I'll feel safer if I'm not out there alone."

Now I'm obligated to go!

"Okay, okay." I also look off to the side. Hopefully, that'll make her feel better. I chose a great day to wear swim trunks under my pants. "Let's grab two towels and head out. Hopefully, we'll be the only ones there."

"Yeah." We go to the bathroom to pick up the towels, then head outside into the dark, cloudless night. "Thanks for joining me, Marlon."

"No problem," I reply, but there's a nervous flutter in my chest that makes me dread stepping into the hot tub with her. We enter the fenced pool area and undress. We lay the towels over our clothes and I take out my phone to put on a classic rock playlist to listen to. I set it by the water's edge.

"Nice tunes," Natalie comments, smiling. She looks amazing in a bikini. Aside from her youthful glow, she clearly takes good care of herself. She's delicate but not frail, from what I can see. It wouldn't surprise me if she works out a lot in her free time.

"Thanks."

She slips into the hot tub after turning it on. The jets are going. Her wide smile is contagious, and she's tilted her head back on the round rim of the tub, her eyes closed. "Ahhh, this feels amazing. Come in, Marlon."

I take my last non-swim garment off — my button-up — and as I'm setting it with our belongings, I catch Natalie peeking at me. As soon as I turn to face her, she looks away.

"Haha, don't pretend like you weren't staring."

She squeaks awkwardly, sinking chin-deep into the hot tub. "I wasn't!"

"Liar." I slip into the hot, bubbling water, and sit in front of a powerful jet. The tension leaves my body. Honestly, I'm amazed at how right this feels.

Not the hot tub, per se, but experiencing something good with a sweet person. When Mariah and I were in the Jacuzzi, it didn't feel this perfect.

"You got me," Natalie finally admits, brushing her wet hair behind her ears. She makes eye contact with me, glowing against the pool lights. I can see her body pretty clearly under the water, and my heart starts to race when my eyes tell my penis that it's time to play.

Holding my hands over my waist, I cross my legs and act as normal as possible. "So, you admit it."

"Your abs are impressive." She giggles. My heart melts. "I wish Frank looked like that."

I gulp. My erection keeps trying to push up between my hands. Natalie is too damn beautiful. Why did Dad have to find her before me?

"He used to," I tell her with a grin. "Back when he was my age. But he doesn't look *bad* nowadays."

"I didn't say *that*." Natalie inches closer to me, but she doesn't touch me. She seems to like being close to people when people are around. However, it's clear to me that she respects boundaries and personal space. The only occasion where her actions could have crossed what's considered to be socially acceptable would be her exhibitionist display earlier.

She continues to speak, voice tender, like a hug from a loved one. "I love your dad. He's a sweetheart."

"Even when he's drunk?"

She nods, but her smile falters.

"It's annoying to be the sober one at a party," I add.

"You can say that again," she says, lips falling to a flat line. "Marlon, I'm glad that you're in Frank's life." Her eyes lock on mine, and her voice takes on a serious tone. "He regrets not being there enough when you were a kid."

"I know." A heavy sigh exits my mouth. Goddamn. "At this point in my life, I don't care if he regrets it or not. I just want to have a strong relationship with him now."

"I didn't have a good relationship with my father."

"You didn't?"

Natalie shakes her head, frowning. "Sometimes I'll say that I did, to make people think I'm normal. But my father was a huge freakin' jerk."

"Yet you came out kind."

A siren wails on the road near the condos. It goes past ours, heading north. It takes me away from the conversation, from the beautiful night sky, from the prettier woman sitting with me in hot, frothing water. Then, I place my back against a jet and let it massage my muscles. It puts me closer to her. Our knees touch, and she gasps, moving hers away. This catches me by surprise, yet she returns her knee to mine after one long breath.

"I'm glad you think I'm kind," she says gently, looking down at the water.

"Your charity goals prove it," I point out.

"I guess."

My eyes close as I contemplate what to do. The relative calm of the night is making me long for intimacy. And Natalie — she smells like the fruit punch that was being served on the yacht. I lean my head back and breath steadily, dreaming about holding her hand.

The sides of our thighs are flush against each other. Both of us have our arms crossed. But as soon as I feel her arms break that rigid form, I reach beneath the water to hold her hand. She says nothing as I feel along her left forearm, fingers dancing on her silky skin before finding her wrist and, finally, threading neatly between hers.

For a few minutes we merely breathe side by side, relaxing in each other's presence. My heart skips a beat when her head rests against my shoulder. Her left side leans on my right side, and her breath matches mine.

"Marlon," she starts, her hesitance plain to my ears. "I like you."

My hand squeezes hers in a comforting manner. Inside, I'm shouting at the universe for putting me in this situation: I can admit it to myself now. I can scream it at the sky.

I am in love with my dad's fiancé.

"For the record," she adds, "I'll never see you as my 'son-in-law'. I'm younger than you are."

I laugh at that. "You know, I'll never see you as my 'mother-in-law'."

She glances up at me, beaming. The blue lights make her look magical. "But I also don't see you as a 'brother-in-law'. You're my friend."

And just like that, I die a little inside.

I know, Marlon, I know. *She's engaged* and it's to my *father*.

Whatever. I'll take friendship. It's better than me being paranoid about if she's using Dad or not.

But friendship means I can't take her right here in this hot tub. Her smell, her looks, her calming voice ... I wonder what she's like on the inside. Unlike with anyone I've been with in the past, I also want to know what she would be like beyond sex. What does she want in the future? Would she like kids? Dogs? A white picket fence?

"I ... should go to bed."

"Okay." Natalie stands up and we leave the hot tub together. "Walk me home?" she says, wide eyes full of hope as she looks at me.

I nod. "Of course."

For her, I'm happy to oblige.

Chapter 10: The Marriage Deception

Dad and Natalie park their car outside my condo as I'm getting my bags into my car. Natalie steps out from the driver's seat and my dad follows soon after, both tanned with a touch of sunburn, wearing shorts and not looking ready to leave.

"Marlon!" Natalie hurries toward me with a big smile on her face. Her sunglasses are pushed up on her head, so I can see her green eyes. "It's sad our vacation's ending, isn't it?"

I raise an eyebrow at her. A quick glance at Dad tells me he's pleased with the two of us, who are getting along so well now. Sharing Natalie's smile, granted mine is more reserved, I say, "it's a bummer, but we'll all get together again soon. Won't we?"

"Of course," Dad says, standing next to Natalie. He wraps an arm around her shoulder and she relaxes against him. "Drive safely and that meeting will be a guarantee. Right, Marlon?"

"Haha, right. You've got nothing to worry about, Dad. I'm a great driver."

Grinning wickedly, Dad says to Natalie, "This kid — when he had his learner's permit, he backed into my car. *While parking in the driveway.*"

There's a new tension in my forehead. I rub at my brow to make it go away. Natalie giggles, then teases, "No way — Little Marlon did *that?*"

"That's right. When I was younger." I laugh, and throw the last of my bags in the back seat of my car, shutting the door right after. Taking the car keys out of my pocket, I open the driver's side and slide in.

"Don't take it personally," Dad chuckles, walking up to the door and placing his hand on the top of it, so I won't close it. He gives me a fatherly look — I swear, I've seen him make that proud-but-worried look a million times while training under him, but only this once in such a casual environment. He's always been the most dad-like at work.

"What is it?" I ask. Maybe I come off as too serious? Natalie's taking a step back and looking a bit concerned. "It was a joke," I say, wanting to ease the tension. "I know that. I'm not offended, guys. Just getting ready to sign out at the main building does the road."

For a moment, I'm certain that Dad is going to demand that I stay here and have a long conversation about my driving abilities or Natalie's charity and the potential partnership it'll have with Whitmer Real Estate. But, to my surprise, he takes his hand off the door and moves back from the car.

"I'm behind you," he says coolly, yet I notice there's a hesitance in his voice. "Call you soon, kid. Stay safe."

"You too."

Dad walks toward his car and Natalie musters a smile, giving a final wave of goodbye before joining my dad in his recently washed car. As soon as they pull out, I leave too. It doesn't take long for me to sign out and drive off from the condo. I can't say this was the best vacation I've ever had — it wasn't by a longshot. But, I'm not disappointed. Even if Mariah was a bust, I got to know Natalie better, and that's what Dad wanted out of this. I'm sure he's pleased. And I've gotta say, I am too.

*

I pull into a small parking lot of a popular coffee shop, Grind It, on the drive back. I'm in a familiar area that runs along this highway. It's part of a small town, which a lot of hipsters and drug dealers make their own. Stepping out of my car, I lock it and head into the small shop. It has a pink neon sign and brick walls painted black on the inside. Large white photos of coffee beans and cups with steaming hot joe offset the dark walls. Honestly, it's nicer than the coffee places near where I live, and if I had to downgrade my living situation, I would consider moving to this mid-Californian town for Grind It alone.

There aren't too many people inside here right now. So, I get in line and place an order of a large hot coffee with two shots of cream and a shot of espresso.

As I'm waiting for my order to-go, smelling ground coffee beans and cherry pastries in the air, I spot a man walking out from the bathroom out of the corner of my eye. When I give him a better look, my eyes go wide and a smile breaks out on my face.

"Dave!" I step toward him — he's standing behind a short Asian woman and a very tall man who looks like he plays in a jazz band. They seem to be a couple.

Anyway, Dave says, "Marlon!" in response to me, and continues with, "It's been a long time. Last time I saw you, you tried selling me a house."

"You would have been my favorite customer if you bought."

Dave chuckles. "You could've given me a better deal." He's slightly overweight, and wears the casual attire of someone who eats at cheap restaurants. "What brings you to Grind It?"

"Just driving back from a trip with my dad and his fiancé."

"Frank's engaged?"

"Yep."

"Good for him. I hope he's happy."

"He is. I'll tell him you said that — I'm sure he remembers our golf outing."

Dave's face turns a little pink. "Yeah, I bet. I shot a golf ball straight into the windshield of his Porsche."

"He liked you, though."

"I know ... and you did more damage to that car than me, didn't you?"

My face heats up with embarrassment. Didn't that minor accident come up earlier with Dad and Natalie? I change the subject. "Whatever — I want to know what you've been up to, David 'Letterman'. In high school, you were the king of the field, out there playing football. You dropped it in college, if I remember. Why was that?"

Dave crosses his arms and says in the friendly manner that I recall from our youth, "My parents convinced me to focus on academics, not sports. Yeah, I might've been good in high school, but I didn't seek scholarships for it. I also couldn't see myself playing football into my fifties, and with the risk of injury cutting that profession short, I figured I would have more money for longer if I got a job that wouldn't give me concussions."

"Fair enough." I pat his shoulder. He tells me to wait a second as he makes his order. I go to check on mine and see that the coffee has been sitting at pick-up for a minute. I grab it and start drinking. The couple that ordered before Dave already have their drinks and Danishes, which they're enjoying at one of the round tables in the dining area.

When Dave comes back, he starts us on another conversation: "How's the love life? You never got married?"

I shake my head. "Well, it's been better, it's been worse. Just ended a fling with a woman who turned out to have a crap personality."

"Sorry, Marlon. That's rough."

"We weren't *together* long. I'm glad that it's done, whatever we had. Anyway, you're happily married. Tell me about Jane."

He lights up at the mention of his wife. "Jane's doing great. She's teaching at a Montessori school, and she loves it there."

"And the kids — tell me about them. Little Josh and Bella."

"Josh just turned seven. He's a menace, but cuter than a button. Jane and I are thinking of putting him in soccer, so he can tire himself out after school. Maybe then he won't draw on the walls."

"Haha, he takes after you then. Weren't you a rambunctious kid?"

"I sure was. But Bella? She's a sweetheart, and the calmest kid I've ever met. I think all the meditation Jane and her do together helps with that. Bella might just be five, but she's already wiser than Josh and some of her older cousins. She'll be even more brilliant when she enters grade school."

"That's great to hear." I mean it, too.

Dave's coffee comes out and he nurses it as we stand near the exit.

"I've gotta ask," I say. "Do you miss your days as a bachelor?"

A mischievous grin crosses his face. "I was wild back in those days. I guess there are times when I miss it — it wasn't stressful in the ways my life is stressful now, 'cause of all the responsibilities."

He gives me a look of compassion, and it feels like he's seeing me as his old self. I don't know how to feel about that, but I might be assuming a lot about how he sees me. He continues.

"And the hookups were fun too. But there's nothing like a stable relationship and having kids. You see yourself in them, and your wife, if she's the right one, makes you feel warm and safe. We're told that emotions aren't that important, that we just need to work and have money. But that's all wrong. The people who tell us that — they don't have what I have with Jane. They don't love their kids like I love mine. I would die for Bella and Josh. I would die for Jane. I feel fulfilled, and I don't feel alone."

"Right, right. I'm glad you're where you're at in life."

"And Marlon, you might know what I mean — the bachelor life is lonely. Cold. Loveless." Dave sighs, and shakes his head. "Life is hard, but love makes it easier. Love is work, don't get me wrong, but it's worth it."

My mind goes to Natalie. I try to push her to the back of my brain. "We ought to talk more," I say. "I have to go. Work and all."

"I'll hit you up later. Nice talking to you, Marlon. Have a safe drive and tell Frank I said hi!"

"Thanks. Have a great week. Tell the wife and kids I wish them well."

I leave. When I get into my car and back onto the highway, I find myself thinking about my parents.

The more I consider it, the worse I feel. My dad should have loved my mother like he loves Natalie. He should have loved me like a son and not an eventual business partner. If I have kids, I want to be like Dave. I want to be involved in their lives from start to finish.

Mom loved Dad until she didn't. When he told her goodbye for the last time — that was what killed her. He broke her spirit and made her life hard. And her health suffered too. As I kid, I saw her bent over, crying because her back hurt from cleaning. She had a business brain like my father, but she lost her job when I was ten, and we were living off of child support for a while. She got a job cleaning houses.

A while ago, she died of cancer. My guess is she was exposed to carcinogenic chemicals while working as a cleaner. I know Dad didn't want her dead, and he didn't want her to be depressed and working her hands to the bone, but he refused to be a father until I was old enough to serve him in some way at work. I'm glad he isn't all about work now, but I would be lying if I didn't hate him for that.

And I don't want my future family to hate me.

Chapter 11: The "Work" Place

Back at work, life is back to its normal pace. It seems that the real estate business isn't in the shitter right now, and we're finally getting more jobs to do. As the CEO, I can't say I'm like a salesman anymore, going out there into the big, wide world trying to get people to buy homes they'll never pay off in full. But I like to do the overseeing of our sales managers, the overseers of the salespeople.

Tonya has been talking to me more. Every time she sways into my office, she brings a bright smile with her. This woman has the whitest teeth I've ever seen on anyone, period.

"I'm going to get coffee on my lunch break," Tonya says, popping in. She's wearing a pink dress and has her black curls pulled up high on her head. Some ringlets fall down around her brown forehead in a cute way. "Want me to get you one?"

"Sure, Tonya. Thanks for the offer." I give her my coffee order and she walks back to her desk — I guess her lunch break isn't for a few minutes, but it's coming up soon enough. I can already taste the coffee.

But not long after Tonya has dropped by, Mariah pays me a visit. It isn't a pleasant one.

While we've tried to act professional since the trip, one of us always falters in some way. Yesterday, I almost kissed Mariah when she leaned over my desk in a particularly revealing blouse to inform me that one of our managers below plans to retire soon and we'll be working with a new fellow who came from Colorado and yada yada — I made a sincere effort to pay attention to her words. But her body is coffee, and while there's a definite benefit to the rush of drinking it, too much might give me a heart attack.

Today — I don't know why this is the case — Mariah is the first to lose her professionality.

She leans over my desk after shutting the office door and moves her arms closer together, elbows on the table, on my paperwork. It makes her breasts stick out more, and in the lower-cut blouse she's in today, I can see clear as day half of one of her rosy nipples peeking out from her jet-black bra.

Shit. I look up at her eyes and lean far back in my chair. Maybe I'm the unprofessional one here after all?

"Hey, Boss," she starts, eyes half-lidded and lips pulled into a devious grin. A shiver runs down my spine when she leans a bit further over the desk.

She's bad news, I think, but my dick is getting hard anyway.

"You've been talking to Tonya a lot."

I raise an eyebrow at her, then I sit up straight. I'm the boss here, damn it. I should be able to keep my employees in check, including the hot ones who I've slept with.

"Yes, Mariah, she *is* my employee."

I watch nervously as Mariah reaches over and takes the pen I was holding out of my hand. She begins to casually chew on the top, her red lips opening enough to let her wet, pink tongue poke out in a playful gesture.

"*I'm* your employee," she says, very quietly.

I run a hand through my hair and nod my head. "That's true, but ... where are you going with this, Mariah?"

She just looks at me. The rest of her movements freeze, like a cat that's caught right as it was about to knock over a vase. I wonder if she's about to inform me that HR will be here any minute to launch an investigation into me.

But that doesn't happen.

Instead, another fear of mine gets checked off the list.

She says, "meet me in the parking lot after work," then walks out.

She doesn't wait for my response, she doesn't explain why she wants us to meet, she merely stands up straight again and *walks out without so much as a glance back*.

Pulling my phone out, I scroll through the newsfeed. I don't think I have many options in regards to seeing Mariah in the parking lot, since we're out at the same time, and avoiding her might be a firing-sentence for me. The best I can do now is distract myself from what's sure to be bad news, with social media and scientific articles about water found on Mars.

After I finish reading an article on the aforementioned subject, I open my social media app, Insta, go look at who I've follows on my one and only fake, private account and voila, I've only followed one person under my profile "UsualGuy", and that person is Natalie.

While Tonya has been on my mind as of late, Natalie hasn't left it since before that terrible trip with Mariah. I hate to admit that I've been acting like a stereotypical teenage chick for a week now, but I *may* have been internet-stalking Natalie. She has a private and public profile, and she only added me to the private account three days ago. I'm really just trying to understand her better, from a distance. When we're too close, it gets uncomfortable, if not all-around disappointing.

For the next few hours, all I can do is try to organize my thoughts and paperwork. I haven't liked a single one of Natalie's pictures, in case doing so draws her attention. She doesn't respond to comments much on her personal profile — under her well-taken selfies lots of men add red hearts or "u r beautiful" and she only likes these comments, while she'll respond to most of the women on her posts who I assume she's friends with or has met in-person.

On the public profile, where she discusses her charity concept and has clearly been doing some marketing for, she'll reply and like all comments, with the exception of a few spam responses. She has quite a following on the public profile — over 5k — compared to the 358 who follow her private. I'm impressed, honestly. She knows what she's doing, from the looks of it.

Between five and six PM, my phone rings, and I answer it: it's Dad. We exchange a brief greeting, then he gets down to business.

"Have you thought more about sponsoring Natalie's charity?"

"I have," I say, reclining on my chair. "I have to ask a few people at work about what they think, but as soon as we determine if it'll work, I'll let you know."

"Natalie is excited about all of this. Well. I'm out playing golf with some of my old friends. I was wondering if you want to come visit us soon. Maybe next week? I'm having a barbecue."

"Sure, that sounds great. What day are you having it?"

"Next Sunday."

"Next Sunday it is, then."

The call ends and I take a deep breath. The work day is about to end. I gather my belongings as everyone else is leaving or has already left, and walk down to the parking lot where I head straight toward my car.

Mariah is leaning against the driver's side door. I gulp — she has her arms crossed, pushing her breasts up. The look on her angular face is serious, though by the way her lower lip sticks out a little I think she might be trying to pout at me. "I want to speak with you in private," she says, getting off my car and stepping toward me with a fire in her eyes. "About the trip and about Tonya."

"So, you haven't gone to HR?"

"Not yet. But if you don't come to my place to discuss this, I'll have to go to them. If that's the only way you'll listen to me, then sure. But I want to give you a chance to right this. You embarrassed me, Marlon."

"Fine, I'll go to your place to talk," I tell her, giving in. "But I want to take my car."

"Sure. Follow me." She starts to walk toward her car, as the evening sky darkens, night drawing in.

Chapter 12: Be Mine — Or Else

Mariah's house is small and devoid of life. There's not even a cat!

Then again, as she leads me into a living room that's covered in wine decor and postcards from friends who live in other countries, like Switzerland. The whole place smells like sandy beaches from a candle she has burning on a granite kitchen counter. The lights in the room all have a pink tint to them, adding to her bachelorette aesthetic. She pours herself a glass of red wine, then pours a second and gestures toward a purple couch in her small living room.

"Take a seat," she says. I do, then she joins me and hands me one of the wine glasses. "Drink up."

"Thanks," I reply, and take a sip. It's cheap.

She sits back against the arm of the couch, drinking. I look at her as she watches me in silence.

"You want to talk about the trip and Tonya," I remind her. Has she forgotten what she invited me here for?

A minute passes. Then, she finally shares what's on her mind. "I don't want you dating in the workplace."

My eyes widen at this. I need another sip. "Excuse me?"

"It's an embarrassment."

I pause, and think about it. If I give her the benefit of the doubt, I can understand how that would be embarrassing. If not embarrassing, I understand that it might upset her to know that I, an ideal man in her eyes I presume, is getting with another woman whom she works with. Then again, we're adults, and I have to question the validity of this request.

She continues emphatically, her legs pressed together, yet angled toward me. I get the sense that she wants me to look at her smooth skin; I admired her softness when we were "together." "You're the boss," she says, "and I'm *beneath you* in the workplace. You having sex with me was totally inappropriate—"

"Stop right there. What we did was consensual."

"Do you think HR will believe that?" Mariah scoffs.

Then, kicking her high-heels off, she places her bare feet up on the couch. First close to her body, then one slides into the crevice between the back cushions and seating cushions. Her leg winds up against my side, with her foot on my butt. The move is aggressive and takes me aback.

"What do you want?" I ask her bitingly.

A devilish look crosses her face, and she suddenly brings her foot up over my thigh, then down between my legs. I raise my eyebrows, letting out a gasp. This can't be true, after I allegedly "embarrassed" her.

"I want you to date me."

My jaw drops. The nerve of this woman!

"I want you to buy me whatever I want. I want you to make love to me *whenever I want*. And ..." She lets out a deep, evil chuckle. I feel like I'm the tin soldier getting a regrettable hard-on for the Wicked Witch of the West. "You live *here*, with me."

"You're crazy!" I shoot off the couch and shatter the wine glass on the floor.

She follows after me, only she purposefully throws her glass on the ground in front of my feet. Glaring at me, Mariah spits out, "If you refuse to see me — and that's *me only* — not only will I tell HR about our encounters: I'll let Tonya know everything that happened on the trip."

"What?"

Somehow, that's worse than me losing my job. Mariah is threatening to ruin my social standing, and not just with a woman I'm mildly interested in: with *everyone at work*. And word spreads.

I feel myself tense up. My jaw clenches.

"You're insane," I say in a lower tone, taking a step back.

She begins to unbutton her blouse, and I gulp. My pants are tented with a raging erection, brought on by adrenaline and, admittedly, sexual attraction.

"Fine, I'll go along with your ridiculous demands." I step forward, asserting myself as the man in charge, though I'm worried that she might mentally break if I take my dominance too far and she'll attempt to stab me in my sleep. "I'll live here, I'll 'date' you — but I won't enjoy either. I'll fuck your brains out, but I won't picture you while we're having sex."

"Let me guess, you'll picture Natalie."

I shut my mouth.

She takes this as an opportunity to grab me by the tie and pull me down into a kiss. She bites my lip, making me moan. "Fine, you can even *call* me Natalie," she whimpers as I grab handfuls of her hair and shove her, her legs apart, onto the couch where I grind into her. "But I get to shame you for it."

"Go ahead," I breathe into her ear, reaching down to grab her hips. I move her against me, making her cry with pleasure. Sick, sick pleasure. "Nothing you say will make me feel more shame than what I already feel. This is my lowest, thanks to you." I unzip my pants and whip out my cock.

Reaching down, I rip Mariah's panties off in one swift motion and shove myself deep into her hot, juicy pussy. "And because you got me here" — I thrust hard, yet keep my rhythm slow, making her quake, and her fingers dig into my back, a voiceless plea for me to keep going — "I'm going to make you pay."

Chapter 13: Dad's Intentions

We spent the whole night fucking. I don't know how I peel myself out of bed the next morning, but I manage. When I turn the bedside lamp on, my eyes burn and a sharp headache comes on.

A hangover. That sucks. Sitting at the edge of the bed, I sigh deeply. The room smells like red wine. Glancing back, I see that Mariah is lying harmlessly in bed, asleep, her back turned toward me.

I don't like being in Mariah's house. I thought that *I* live alone — this place is dreary. The decor she's placed in her bathroom, totaling a strange horse painting across from the gray shower curtains and a fake gold vase with dried lavender sticking out of it, doesn't do much to brighten the place.

I take a shower, trying to wash away the shame from last night and this new arrangement I'm stuck in. The thought of being with Mariah, as sexually stimulating as she is, is verifiably nightmare fuel. Aside from how few hours I slept, the quality of that sleep was atrocious. Now my mind won't stop racing with fantasies about Natalie, of us going behind my dad's back to hook up. I dreamt that I had a child with Mariah, and I ended my life because it was supposed to be Natalie's.

This is all wrong. Honestly, my longing for Natalie aside, I could never be with Mariah, especially since I've seen the way she lives, a life that lacks companionship in any sincere form and a terrible taste in interior design. No wonder she wants riches, the superficial toys people like my dad — and myself if I was inclined — purchase for show only to later dispose of. A model plane, a gold cap, a spot on Elon Musk's trip to Mars, etc.

"Mariah."

I jostle the woman awake. She rolls over, naked in the sheets, and blinks herself awake. A drowsy groan escapes her, then a coy smile is formed by her lips, which are bruised from hours of rough sex.

"My dad made plans with me for me to go to his place tonight, for dinner. You wouldn't mind if I go alone, would you?"

For a moment, Mariah seems to process my request. Her smile slowly dies, and her eyes catch cold. "Who's going to be there, Marlon?"

I consider my response carefully. I spent the night calling Mariah "Natalie" when I wasn't *being a dick* to her, since the fantasy I had playing in my head — an attempt to escape the strange reality that I've come to find myself in — involved me dicking my dad's fiancé with love, not the genuine hatred I feel for Mariah.

Given that Mariah got jealous of Tonya when I did little more than speak to our coworker with evident interest in Tonya's personal life, I think it's better to lie.

"Only my dad will be there. Natalie is out of town with some friends."

"Oh," Mariah rolls her eyes. "Those 'friends' of hers she told us about."

"Yeah, those friends. The ones who like her creativity. Anyway, can I go?"

She told me last night, after I made her cum a second time, that I can't see anyone without her permission. Tomorrow, she wants me to move in. I don't know how I'll explain that to my landlord. I'm pretty certain I can't go through with it, but I may have to fake agreeing to all of her demands until I'm able to figure out how to get her not to talk with HR.

"With me?" she asks, staring at me intently.

I inwardly grimace. The thought of bringing her to my dad's place is genuinely horrifying. I would almost rather lose my high-paying job than go through that embarrassment.

"Not with you, since he doesn't like you."

Mariah's face turns red at this, but she doesn't say anything at first. "Your father doesn't like *me*? Wow. How can you see him, if he doesn't like me?"

Hopefully, getting her pissed off alone won't warrant an HR visit. "He's my dad, and he's stuck with me through most of my life. And if

I don't go tonight, alone, he'll think something is wrong. Hell, he may call the police."

Obviously, I'm exaggerating, but Mariah, in her jealousy-catalyzed possessive fugue state, doesn't seem to know this.

"Fine, go alone," she sighs, shaking her head.

*

Later, I arrive at Dad's house, pulling into his driveway and feeling a sense of freedom that I haven't felt since I left work just yesterday.

As per usual, dad has been waiting near the front windows in the dining room across from the front entrance. He walks out with Natalie in tow. Both wear casual clothing, like they've been taking a break from life for a while: matching gray sweatpants and blue hoodies. I can't help but laugh at how silly it is, when couples match outfits. I'm grinning when I leave my car and go to hug them both.

"Nice to see you," I say, hugging Dad.

He pats my back, saying, "Nice to see you too. I'm glad you could make it."

Natalie hugs me next, and it's a gentle hug. There's a light in her eyes when she looks closely at my face that makes me think she may have been wanting to see me a lot. "Thanks for coming," Natalie says. There's a general softness to her today that's quite the relief for me, what with all the intense and borderline painful interactions that I had with Mariah last night.

We go inside and sit in their spacious living room. Natalie has added green plants to spice up the place, some succulents hang from the walls by green art nails and potted tropical flora sat symmetrically by the glass back doors. Natural light pours in, while the ceiling lights produce a soft white glow that doesn't hurt the eyes.

I think that Natalie's touches to this mansion have made it homier. If I didn't have my own place right now, or Mariah demanding that I move in with her, I might ask Dad if a son can have a room here for himself.

Natalie takes a seat on Dad's knee after he's planted himself on a leather recliner across from the matching leather couch I'm sitting on. He holds her close, wearing a pleasant expression as he does so.

"So, Marlon, what's it like being back at work with your ex?"

Ah, so he's getting straight to business. "Not bad, but you know."

"I know?" he repeats, confused.

"Yeah, you know how it goes with women in the workplace."

"I'm not sure that I do."

"Me neither," Natalie laughs out loud, perhaps with some discomfort.

I press my lips together, before letting myself relax into the couch cushions. They're not especially soft, but there's a quilt behind me that helps.

"Come on, you two. Don't make me explain what it's like."

"Just answer this," Dad says. "Do you regret taking Mariah on our trip?"

"Easy answer. Of course I do."

My dad chuckles and shakes his head. Natalie smiles, but she seems less humored by my response. A sympathetic look falls over her, while Dad slaps his knee at my discomfort.

"I could have told you *that* from a mile away."

"Frank," Natalie starts, sounding serious, "you definitely *couldn't*."

He shrugs. "Well, *you know*. Maybe it's just the way I feel in retrospect."

Natalie turns to me and frowns. "I'm sorry, Marlon. If it makes you feel any better, I thought she was beautiful, and beauty can be deceiving; it can hide a bad personality for a while." She adds with a little enthusiasm, "One of my friends dated a man for *six months*, because of how attractive he was to her. She ended it, though, because it would never get serious in a way she felt comfortable with. This guy took her to meet his parents, let them embarrass her at a family brunch, went to *her* parents' house and made a fool of himself with his heavy drinking, and he completely forgot her birthday and told her she was gaslighting him about when she was born. *Because he didn't want to make it up to her.*"

"That's pretty bad," I commented.

Natalie nods. "Exactly. But if you were to look at the guy, personality wouldn't be your first thought. It would be his eight-pack and the flaccid bulge in his pants."

"Is that all women want these days?" Dad asks, giving Natalie a tickle, which makes her fidget and giggle.

"No, no," she replied, fidgeting until he relents. "Women want love and support. Connection. Fun."

"Mariah wants money," I say, feeling myself die inside at the thought of spending another second in that crazy woman's house. Why can't Natalie be with me instead? She's a real goddamn person!

"Money ruins lives, I swear." Natalie smirks at my dad. He scoffs in a humored manner, raising an eyebrow at his good fiancé.

"You lost the right to say that," Dad teases.

"Have I?"

"After today, you do."

"What do you mean?" I ask, curious.

Natalie's mouth opens in feigned, shocked offense. Her gaze goes between me and Dad before landing on me. "I was going to save that news for dinner."

"What news?" I inquire.

"The good news."

For a moment, it feels like I'm going to have a heart attack. I don't show it, but I feel like she's just carved me with a knife. Is she pregnant? Is she starting a family with my remaining family? If she is, there's no chance that I'll ever be with her. She can't be birthing my half-brother! That's some Oedipus Rex shit, and I'm not into it!

"It's about my charity," she specifies after those few seconds of my panic. "Oh, Frank, now the surprise is basically ruined. You're a surprise-ruiner."

"Surprise-ruiner?" Dad pulls her in and makes her squeal. It's cute, but I want to be the one pulling her close. It's just wrong, their love. "I didn't say what the surprise was, now did I?"

It only feels natural for me to contribute to the discussion. "What? Did you get your charity registered and now you're in business?"

Natalie gasps and looks wide-eyed at me. A second passes, then she asks in disbelief, "Who told you?"

"It was a guess!" I laugh hard, delighted for her but also embarrassed that my guess was spot-on. I took her surprise away. "I'm sorry, Natalie. I hope this doesn't ruin dinner."

"No, it doesn't," she says through cute giggles, "it just makes the telling of it less fun. Whatever. I'm working with five others who graduated in the same class as me at college to put together a workplace at this building Frank is renting for me."

Dad smiles at me, and I can't help but return the look of joy. "Best investment I ever made," he says.

"Congratulations!" I reach across toward their chair, to give her a fist-bump. She takes me up on that offer and beams in my direction. "I'm happy for you. I mean it."

We eat dinner in great moods, all smiles and great talk. After I leave, I spend my drive thinking about how I'm going to get Mariah out of the picture. She complicates my life, and my life is already complex.

Then, an idea hits me. It might take time, but I'll get rid of Mariah.

Chapter 14: How To Save Myself

Two months have gone by. Natalie's charity is up and running, and the economy is getting better. Problem is, Mariah is still here — my grand idea was to get her transferred to another branch of Whitmer Real Estate, in Oregon, but I have to get her transferred secretly, so she won't be tempted to report me — and I've been living with her for weeks. Miserable weeks.

She's acting worse now, too. Natalie, always a beam of sunshine in my life, comes into my workplace frequently, since we're now in business together. Sponsoring her charity has been great, and I feel like a better man for doing this: we're helping to house the homeless and, on the side, Natalie's charity has figured out a way to use pets — most are from shelters that would have put them down if it wasn't for us — to improve the quality of lives of people who wouldn't otherwise be able to keep a therapeutic animal companion around. Whitmer Real Estate is the perfect partner for this charity, and I personally bought an apartment complex with a little money I had saved up to convert it into a pet-friendly, low-rent living space for those who aren't fit to work.

Whenever Natalie is around, Mariah goes insane. More insane than what she usually is, that is.

She's a bitch to me, and will avert her eyes if Natalie ever looks her way. I swear, she put laxatives in my coffee yesterday, to punish me for having Natalie come in. Here I thought Mariah was giving me a treat that wouldn't make me shit my brains out for multiple hours. I had to miss a company call because of it. I'm thankful that Mariah hasn't realized I've been calling the Oregon branch trying to work out a transfer, because I think she would do more than talk with HR.

The sex, I have to admit, is better than ever, because she's insane and that adds to the excitement of whatever we do in bed — I think the threat of her grabbing a knife she keeps under her pillow to kill me if I don't obey her makes sex hardcore on a psychological level.

The good news is, I'm due to speak with the manager of the Oregon branch. I just sent him an email agreeing to this meeting. They are interested in inviting her over for a leadership position.

Chapter 15: Away

"Harder, harder, Boss!"

I hold Mariah's head down on the bed, as she requested. She only likes it rough, which is honestly exhausting. Nevertheless, she has a great ass, and I get to spank it with my free hand, turning her cheeks red as I pound into her, feeling the end of my cock hit a notch whenever I push in all the way to the hilt.

Thank God there aren't any neighbors nearby to hear Mariah's ear-piercing moans and screams. Her eyes roll into the back of her head as I go harder and faster into that used, loose pussy. I grab one of her ass cheeks as I pant and sweat with each thrust, placing my thumb, slick with her juices, right next to that bleached, puckered anus of hers.

"Aaaah! Put it in! Put it in!" She shoves her ass back against me and my thumb slips into her cleaned-out rectum. Her body quivers as I finger her butthole, all the while thrusting deep inside her, going raw because she won't allow condoms.

I have to squeeze my eyes shut to forget who I'm with. When I close my eyes, I picture Natalie in her place; I'm fingering Natalie's perfect ass, pounding her tight, hot hole, making her cry out in pleasure and drool on the sheets, making her eyes roll as I carefully but firmly yank her head by the hair.

Mariah's vagina pulses when she climaxes, and she squirts on the towel we've laid under her. I keep going, wanting badly to cum but also fearing the consequences.

She starts to gasp and quiver when I don't stop. "Please, please, Marlon, it's too much!"

Not our safe word — that would be "bird".

"No, it's not, you can take this." I grab her hip with the hand I had been using to hold her head down with, and with my slick left hand, I shove more fingers into her ass, stretching it out. "I want to cum this time. Damn it, bitch, let me cum in your ass!"

Mariah goes limp on the bed, letting out a continuous moan. The sheet by her face is wet with drool. Her mouth is open, tongue hanging out like a dog on a summer day.

Her walls stop pulsing, and I'm happy to pull out of her unbelievably wet pussy. It's lubed my cock up enough that when I shove myself deep into her well-stretched ass, she only lets out a small, needy whimper.

Then, Mariah's phone rings. We ignore it, and she gasps when my clean hand plays with her clit, while my dick slips in and out, in and out of that fantastic ass. I squeeze my eyes shut and groan — I see white, and all the pressure within me, especially in my balls, shoots out in a powerful cumshot. I ride it out, moaning along with her, then when I pull out and collapse on my back on the bed, Mariah drags herself to the top of her bed, where she reaches over in the dim lighting of her bedroom to grab her phone and answer the call.

"Hello, Mariah speaking."

My ears ring too loudly for me to hear the contents of the call. I nearly pass out; I feel so lightheaded and all-around light from orgasm. It's a workout, pleasing this evil woman on the bed with me.

When my vision and hearing returns to normal, I glance over at Mariah and see her set her phone on the bedside table. She looks happy, and tells me, "That was the head of the Oregon branch. He wants me to drive over for an interview a week from now."

"Congrats!" I give her a loveless kiss on the leg. Are these horrors about to end? "Think you'll take it?"

She hesitantly looks at me with her dark, penetrating eyes. "I was told to think it over and call back in a few days to confirm."

Okay. "Do you want the job, though?"

Again, she seems to consider her response carefully. "The job sounds great, and would be better than my current position, but I don't really want to go."

That's what I was afraid of. "Why not?"

"My life is here. *You're* here."

Oh no.

"That's true, but just think about it, okay?"

How will I make her *want* to leave?

*

I drive up to my dad's house for dinner. Mariah let me leave without giving me a hard time today, probably because she's considering alternative living situations now that she has the option to move to Oregon. She hasn't decided if she'll do the interview yet, but I've been thinking hard on what to do, so I haven't given up hope yet.

At the dinner table, Natalie pulls up a video on her phone and shows it to me and Dad. The smell of barbecued ribs hangs in the air, sweet and tangy. Somehow, this video distracts me from the meat, and I'm treated to Natalie and some of her girlfriends in dresses, speaking with an interviewer in a small but colorful room, on round seats that remind me of dandelions.

"This has gotten so many hits," she says, pointing at the view count at the bottom of the screen. It's well over fifty-thousand.

The TV ads, to my knowledge, have helped with the charity's success. It hasn't been around for long, so the volume of donations it has received is impressive. Natalie hired a teen to help her with social media promotion, too, since she can afford it now. The charity is feeding itself, it seems, and the more money that's donated to the charity, the more efficiently the charity can run and the more people we can help. I've started making private donations as well.

"I was also interviewed in a really popular magazine. Our analytics team is helping a lot with our marketing. Thanks for finding them for me, Frank."

Natalie smooches my dad on his lips. I keep my eyes locked on the phone, wishing that she had given me that kiss.

We get back to eating. Once we're done, we go outside on Dad's patio and watch the sunset in the west. The three of us sit together on a cushioned swing-chair. We've lit Tiki torches to brighten up the place in the face of darkness.

Natalie and Dad sit close to each other, holding hands. I sit across from them. For a while, we discussed politics. Now, I don't know what their inaudible whispers mean.

Then, they make it clear.

"Lonny," my dad says with a wide grin, "next month, Natalie and I are tying the knot."

A chill washes over me.

Taking in a deep breath, I lean back and close my eyes. My brain spins from the oncoming loss of Natalie to Mariah waiting for me back at her home. I dread leaving, and now I dread confronting these two about how I feel regarding their marriage.

"Congratulations," I eventually mutter. My body feels heavy, and I can't even pretend to be excited.

I think Natalie notices my discontent. Good ol' Frank, however, ignores my minimal response and continues with, "Will you be my best man, Marlon?"

There's a long pause. I have to process this. They've been engaged for so long, I forgot that they might eventually make it official.

"Sure," I say with a slight shrug that I hope he doesn't spot. "Why not? I *am* your son."

"I appreciate it," Frank says.

I don't want to call him my dad anymore. I didn't realize how bitter my heart is until now, and I wish I knew how to handle it. I give Natalie a sad look, and she returns it, obviously concerned for my well-being. It wouldn't surprise me if she's

"You're a great kid, Marlon," Frank adds, perhaps sensing some tension in the air.

I stand up and put my hands in my pockets. "It'll be weird calling you my step-mom, Natalie."

"Just call me by my name," she says softly. Dad gives her ass a squeeze and she gives him an offended look.

"What?" Frank asks snappily, not seeming to realize that the grab was inappropriate for this context.

"I told you to lay off the wine," she snaps back, voice wavering. Frank looks upset, and he crosses his arms. It's then that I notice a familiar blush along his face. I hadn't paid much attention all night, since Mariah was unfortunately on my mind, but now it's plain to see that he's been drinking and within the last few minutes he's crossed into the line of drunkenness.

Natalie begins to cry, and my heart breaks for her. I warned her, hadn't I? She told me herself, how this man isn't perfect, how he drinks too much at times.

"I'm tired," she announces, and it's sudden. Up until now, she's acted lively. "I'm going inside. See you later, Marlon." She doesn't look at either of us. Instead, she hurries into the mansion and disappears inside of it.

I turn to Frank and shake my head at him. "What were you thinking?"

"Don't ask," Frank grumbles, running his hands over his face.

"Seriously, Dad. You need to cut back on alcohol. It's gonna rot your liver."

His glare hits mine for a moment, but soon his face is lowered and I can tell that he's ashamed. An inch of me thinks, "poor guy." The rest of me says, "serves him right."

"I'm gonna go now. But I mean it. Congrats. Natalie's perfect." I turn to leave, but I'm still furious that he would hurt Natalie's feelings. Looking back, but only for a second, I add, "you need to step up your game."

Then, I leave.

As awful as that end to the day was, I learned two important things. First, Natalie may not be satisfied enough with my dad's behavior for her to stick with him until the wedding day.

Second, my dad and Natalie's marriage will save me from Mariah. Key word: mother-in-law.

Chapter 16: Freed From Crazy

At work, Natalie stops by to discuss the wedding. She called me earlier, telling me it would be about our next promotional campaign. But while I'm working in the office, she brings in a scrapbook full of different white dresses, flower sets, ribbons, bows, and silverware sets.

Setting that scrapbook down in front of me, she takes a seat across from mine and asks, smiling, "what do you think?"

"About your wedding plans?" I raise an eyebrow at her. Flipping a few pages over, I scan the magazine cutouts and internally groan. "I'm a man, Natalie. I don't know what will work."

"Oh, come on, you have nice eyes."

I point at the first dress displayed in the scrapbook. "You'll only need one dress. There. That's my advice."

She closes the scrapbook and sighs, wrapping it tightly against her chest. "Frank told me to ask you to help me budget, since you're looking at numbers all the time. I told him I didn't need the extra help, but I did. I don't want an expensive wedding."

"If you don't want an expensive wedding, why not just find a dress, grab some flowers from outside, put 'em in dollar store vases and hold the ceremony in your backyard?"

Natalie's light eyes glimmer as a giggle escapes her. "I don't know, Marlon, that might be *too* cheap. Not just for my tastes—"

Mariah walks in behind Natalie, a look of aggravation plain on her face. I stare at Mariah, who stares at me with eyes fit for a killer. Realizing it's not just the two of us in here, Natalie turns around and gasps.

"Oh! Hi there, Mariah," she says, trying to be polite.

Mariah scoffs at Natalie, placing her hands on her hips. "Marlon, what is she doing here?"

"Well, Mariah, Natalie does business with Whitmer Real Estate. What do you need?"

Her dark eyes flicker down at Natalie, who turns back toward me and folds her hands up on the table.

"I want to talk to you, in private."

"Give us a few more minutes, and we can have that talk."

Mariah relents and backs out of the room, returning to her cubicle directly across from my office. Natalie releases a sigh and runs a dainty hand through her thick, bright hair.

"For a moment, I thought she'd come at me with a pair of scissors," Natalie murmurs.

"I thought so too," I say jokingly, but something inside me considers that as a very real possibility. "I would have stopped her."

"I hope so. Anyway, I really want to get your feedback on the table bouquets." She flips to the right page and gestures at the various bouquet styles glued in the book. "I think that the roses and violets look pretty bundled together, but I don't want any clashing colors. It should all be on-theme; we're doing a woodland fantasy theme. I was hoping that Frank would go for these wildflower bundles, but he doesn't want any lavender for some reason, which has been frustrating me. I think the smell bothers him, but he won't admit that. Like somehow a smell sensitivity makes him less of a man. God."

She folds her arms and leans back in the chair, face turning toward the ceiling, coupled with a groan.

"He shouldn't be giving you a hard time," I say, reaching across the table and pulling the scrapbook close to me.

I pick it up and give the pages a long look. She has a great artistic eye. I'm impressed, if I'm being honest. Maybe I should hire her as a developer, landscaper, or architect in training? Maybe I'll show her to the interior design department?

"I like lavender," I add.

A warm smile crosses Natalie's lips, and she relaxes. "Maybe I should be marrying you."

"Maybe."

We go quiet for a moment. Clearly we're joking, but I think the two of us are getting more of a sense that we might make a better match. Still, Frank is excited for the wedding, and it would be wrong to deny him a woman he loves.

"Regardless of whatever bouquet you go with," I continue, "you'll be the prettiest part of the wedding."

She blushes at averts her eyes. "You flatter me."

I smile at her and shrug, trying to give off a casual vibe, then Mariah walks in again and ruins our fun. Now I'm genuinely afraid she might have lost it.

"You're cheating on me!" she declares, glaring at me and Natalie as she stands in the doorway. A sudden silence replaces the soft buzz of speech out in the cubicles, and I stand up, ready to stop whatever this insanity is in its tracks.

"I'm not cheating on you," I say firmly, asserting myself as the boss of this establishment. "I'm discussing my soon-to-be-step-mother's wedding plans. How *dare* you accuse me of cheating on you *with my step-mom*I And in front of all our coworkers!"

Mariah steps back, a shocked look falling over her. I think she realizes that she went a little far with that loud accusation, and at work too.

"I'm sorry, Marlon, I didn't know—"

"Oh, yes you did. Don't start that with me — I see right through your lies. You ought to treat your new mother-in-law with more respect!"

"I ... I ..." Mariah glances pathetically at Natalie, then at me again. Many eyes, including Tonya's, stare into Mariah's backside. "She won't be *my* mother-in-law! I'm taking the job in Oregon. We're over, Marlon Whitmer!"

Face red with embarrassment, Mariah storms out of my office and screams a quick "shut up!" at our coworkers before getting back to work, which to her at this moment appears to be aggressive online shopping and disconnecting her phone line.

"I'm sorry about that," I say to Natalie, taking my seat. She gives me a dumbfounded look.

"I didn't know you were together again."

I exhale deeply. "I wasn't given many options. She wanted to get me fired for not wanting to see her again."

"That's crazy," Natalie whispers, eyes wide. "Jesus — so, I guess it's a good thing she broke up with you."

"That's right," I reply with a nod. I feel like a weight has been lifted off my shoulders. "The torture is finally over. All I have to do is pick up my stuff from her place. Thank God I kept my lease at the old apartment."

"You've been *living* with her?"

Grimacing, I say, "unfortunately. And let me tell you: it's no mansion."

Later that same day, I drive to Mariah's house to get my belongings. I don't go inside, and I don't see her. She's thrown everything of mine outside, and a few things are missing.

Whatever. I'm happy to be done with this chapter in my life. But now I'm onto another one, and I'm scared that it may get worse.

It might break my heart.

Chapter 17: Untimely Confessions

It's a week before the wedding.

How did we get here?

I'm at my dad's house, sitting with him on the couch. Natalie has been pacing the living room for the last seven minutes, anxiety emanating off her like heat from a furnace.

"We're not inviting anyone on your mother's side," Dad points out matter-of-factly.

"Obviously," I say, wishing that he would realize his disdain for my mother and her family was clear from the divorce.

Natalie goes to water some plants, apparently in an attempt to relax. She mutters something under her breath, and Dad asks her to speak up. Turning toward us on the couch, Natalie says, dark circles under her eyes from restless nights, "You should have sent your invites out four weeks ago."

"Don't get snippy with me," Frank grumbles in response, shaking his head.

Scoffing, Natalie returns to watering her plants.

"Dad," I say, elbowing his arm, "she's right, you know. If I was in your position, I would have had a list made out and invites sent out as soon as we finalized the date."

Frank's blue eyes squint at me. He's balder than he was a few months ago, but I think it's his age and not stress — stress these days just bounces off of him, for Natalie to absorb.

"What do you mean?" he asks.

I stand up and hand him the invitation list and pen he had given me, to help him do his job. He looks at me baffled, like I've somehow betrayed him by not doing his part for the wedding. "All I'm saying is *this* is your fault" — I gesture at the papers and pen on his lap — "and you reap what you sow. Want to get married? Get married. But be a man about it and play your part. Natalie can't do all the work."

"I'm paying for it," Frank states defensively.

I cross my arms. "Are you serious? That's the best you've got? If you think money is all it takes, no wonder you wouldn't stay married to Mom."

Natalie taps my shoulder. I look back at her and see an urgent look in her eyes. Her hair is pulled back in a tight ponytail, and she isn't wearing any makeup — her natural look is just as beautiful, despite a layer of stress around her eyes. She wears a red, loose-fitting flannel, light pink jeans, and brown fuzzy slippers.

"Can I show you my art room?" she asks tiredly. "I want to make a giveaway basket, and one of my paintings will be in it. I just haven't decided which one it'll be."

"Sure, I'll help you out." I shoot my dad a look that says *get your act together* before walking upstairs with Natalie. She takes me down a long, clean hallway and into a room with a tall ceiling and plenty of natural lighting from big, opened windows.

Canvases hang on the walls, or lean against them, some small, some large, some of impressionistic garden scenes and others of children throwing tea parties or adorned with fairy wings and elfin ears. There's some still life too, of fruit baskets and coffee beans, but in each of these paintings one thing is off — a banana fallen from the bowl, many coffee beans spilling over the bag — which makes the still life feel alive and moving. I'm impressed by her creativity and skillful painting, and when I see large sketches of blueprints for remodeling plans of recently bought poor housing, my idea to give her an official position at Whitmer Real Estate is confirmed to be great. I have never met someone so ambitious and thoughtful. Usually, those two qualities cancel each other out: the ambitious step on others to achieve their goals; the thoughtful stay immobile in society, too concerned with maintaining peace and a stable presence to risk anything. Natalie is both, and I love that about her.

And Frank doesn't appreciate that enough about her. It isn't just frustrating now, being in love with my father's fiancé, it's depressing.

He's taking her for granted, just like he did my mom, and I can't accept that. Not at all.

"Marlon," she says, closing the door behind us. "Thank you, for being here for us."

"No problem."

"Remind me, why did Frank divorce your mom?"

I place my hands on her art table and lean against it, head down. My eyes focus on the blueprints. "They weren't meant to be together. When he was born, Dad didn't want to take care of me — he has no capacity for children. He could only bring himself to talk to me when I was a teenager."

"I want kids." Natalie sniffs. I don't look up, however, because I don't want to see her crying. That would be too painful. "Frank doesn't even want us to adopt. I say sperm donation, he says that if he can't be the father, he won't be a father. I mentioned you, Marlon, and he didn't like that. He told me to forget about it. I told him it isn't that easy; I've always wanted kids. He told me we could adopt, but he's gone back on that. He doesn't want the responsibility of a parent."

"Sounds like Dad."

She cries, holding in the louder sounds with her hands over her mouth. I turn to her and hold my arms open, and she steps into my hug. My heart aches for her, not just in love but also in sympathy.

"You're amazing, Natalie. He misled you, if you told you he wasn't against adoption. He's told me before that he wants to be a father, but that's an issue he's always flip-flopped on. It isn't fair of him, and you deserve better than that."

"But I love him, Marlon." Her head rests on my shoulder. Her hands move from her mouth to my back, holding me tightly. I can't see her face, but I can feel her heaving chest and I hear the hurt in her voice. The anger I feel toward Frank grows and grows.

"I love him too."

"I'm tired, Marlon. I don't know what to do. He means so much to me. So much."

I nod, closing my eyes so I can feel closer to her; all I feel and smell and hear is her. "He's stubborn, and he's old."

"But he's more than that. He's so sweet and supportive."

"Do you really want to be with a man who wants no children?"

She whispers, "I don't know, but I'm getting married in a week. That's it."

"Is that really it? You won't stand up for what you want? You'll let your devotion to him get in the way of having a family of your own?" I take her shoulders and hold her back from me, making her look at my face. She's tearful and frowning miserably. "You're an amazing person. You can find someone who will recognize that, and who will also want what you want. Frank had a family, and he chose to get rid of it until he could benefit from it. I worked for that man for years, Natalie. I was a loyal son who wanted to make his dad proud — the father who wouldn't so much as show up to his boy's birthday party, let alone change any diapers or play catch with him. I was that child who didn't have a good relationship with his father growing up. You told me yourself: you also didn't have a good relationship with your dad."

Her gaze falls to my chest and her lips quiver. I move a little closer to her, trying to keep her glossy eyes on my face.

"He's ungrateful, Natalie. He loves you, that's true, but children are a burden to him and even if he sticks around if you get pregnant or adopt, that doesn't mean he'll parent." Her eyes meet mine. She's listening closely. "Natalie, if you go through with this, you can't have kids. You'll have to give that dream up, unless you plan on divorcing him when that time comes, *if* it comes. It's not my place to say go through with it or don't. It's not the son's place to sabotage his father's wedding, or convince the fiancé to leave him. But I consider you my friend, Natalie. You're important to me, Natalie, and it hurts me to see you throw away something you want just to make an old man happy.

You deserve better. He deserves someone great, and he deserves love, but you're not meant for him. You never were, despite how good you are to him and how good he is to you."

"I didn't know you thought so much about this," she says softly, wiping her tears away.

"It's because I care, Natalie. More than you'll ever know."

For a moment, her face comes very close to mine. My heart begins to race. Am I crazy for saying what I've said? Is she starting to assume ... no ... guess accurately, that I'm in love? That I'm the idiot who fell for his father's fiancé?

"If you care that much," she sighs out, "I should have gotten with you instead." A troubled laugh escapes her.

I feel a pit in my stomach. I've never felt it before, but now it's overwhelming. It's almost nauseating, holding my feelings in like this. I have to say it, even if it ruins my relationship with Dad.

"Natalie, I have a confession to make."

"Marlon?"

It's time.

"I'm in love you."

Her eyes widen, startled. Her jaw drops.

"I fell for you a while ago," I confess, surprising myself even — I thought I would feel ashamed, but I'm feeling strangely relieved to say it out loud, to her face. "If I could have a wife, a lifetime partner, a mother to *my* kids, I would want her to be you. I love you, Natalie, and I know we can't be together if you marry my father. That was clear to me from the start."

For a moment, she seems like she wants to say something. But her voice catches in her throat.

"I feel terrible for betraying my father like this, but I didn't choose to love you. I didn't choose this, and it took me a while to accept it. I can't live with myself if I say nothing. I'm sorry." I let go of her and step back, leaning against the table again. "This complicates the wedding more, and you're already stressed to hell with it. But I needed to say it. Selfish, I know. But it had to be done. Again, I'm sorry." My voice cracks when I speak. "I know you don't love me back—"

"I do love you."

What?

My heart thumps hard in my chest.

Did I hear her right?

"I love you, Marlon."

No way.

"It started small, but over the last month, I feel nothing but love for you. I love you, but I also love Frank," she says, uncertainty straining her voice. Her hand touches my shoulder, lightly. "I love you both. I don't know what to do in general about the children issue with Frank. And if I'm being honest, I'm scared. I'm terrified now that I know *you also love me*." Natalie starts to cry again, tears heavier than before. "I don't know what to do, Marlon. I don't know ..."

"Let's sleep on it," I suggest, tears beginning to form in my eyes. I wish I was stronger than this, but I'm stressed out. These tears aren't a choice.

We hug each other. I consider kissing her, but I can't. Not while she's with Frank. I won't do that to my dad. But I want her badly. I want to live with her. I want a life with her. Not just sex, not just company. She can be the mother of my children. She can be my best friend. She can be everything to me.

And we'll give it a night. We'll go our separate ways until I visit again, tomorrow. We'll know what to do by then, I hope. We'll decide then, to marry Frank or leave him for each other.

I wish love was easier than this.

Chapter 18: Unexpected

In my lonely, dark apartment, I slept on it.

On a bed alone, I slept on it.

And while my heart demanded that I tell her to be with me, that I convince her it's in her best interest to leave my father, my conscience convinced me otherwise. Ultimately, she's the one who has to decide, and because I love her, I'll support her decision no matter what.

That's what love means to me.

*

Dad's grilling some ribs for us three out on the patio. Natalie and I sit at the round, iron picnic table, enjoying fruit salad on separate ceramic plates.

"I talked to Frank last night," she whispers to me while said man is deafened by the sizzling meat a few yards away. Natalie wears a green lacy dress, and her hair is down, flowing free and blowing in the wind. "I discussed kids again, and he said he'll reconsider it after the wedding."

"That's a lousy answer," I say pointedly, giving her a long, serious look. My fork absently slides into a large strawberry and some lettuce leaves.

"I know," she replies, her friendly smile falling into a straight line. There's hope in her wide eyes as she glances over at the distracted old man. "The charity is doing well."

"Hm. It is, but would you take the charity over being a mom?"

"The charity is self-sustaining now, basically, so I'll take both."

"In that case" — I frown when I look back at Frank — "think carefully about what you want. He might just be saying that to ensure that you marry him. Once it's on paper, it'll be harder to separate."

A cool wind blows at us.

"An omen," Natalie muses.

My lips press together as I think about what this could mean for her, and for us. "It could be ..."

"Gah!" Dad has set the ribs on a big plate, and he's emptied the rest of a barbecue sauce bottle. "I have to go to Smoke Superior to get more of this. Is that okay, guys? I gotta drive — it's twenty minutes away. The only place where this brand is sold, you know."

"It must be costly," Natalie says.

"Fifty bucks a pop!" he laughs in response.

"Yeah, it's fine if you go buy it," I say, "but be careful on the highway. It was high-traffic driving over here."

"I'm better at driving than you are, Marlon. But of course, I'll be careful." He pats my back and gives Natalie a kiss on the head before he leaves. He takes the meat inside, too, to spare us flies with dinner.

"Why not go inside? I'll make us tea," Natalie offers with a smile. She seems eager to get up and make us tea. I accept her offer gratefully and follow her inside. I wait in the kitchen with her as the water comes to a boil in Dad's one and only Chinese tea pot. She pours the water after it's boiled, into two white cups with metal strainers full of tea leaves at the top. The water changes colors, to a tasteful brownish orange.

"Smells like oolong," I comment.

"You're right," she giggles. "This won't be the last time I make tea for you, Marlon."

"Oh, I could have guessed that."

It's nice, I think, for her to take a break from marriage talk and breakup thoughts. Even though it's important that she makes her mind up before the day of the wedding, I can fathom what it's like to be in her position. In a way, it's much worse than mine. And if my position in this love triangle is bad, that says a lot about hers.

My phone rings. I reach into my pocket and answer it.

"Hello," a woman says. "Is this Marlon Whitmer?"

"Yeah. Who's this?"

"I'm Brandy, calling from Northwestern Hospital. Can you verify your date of birth for me?"

My heart pounds and my breath catches in my throat. I tell her my birthdate, and demand why.

"Your father Franklin Whitmer has been in a car accident. He's currently in the emergency room, in critical condition. He's requested that you come to the hospital immediately."

I nearly drop my phone. "We have to go," I say to Natalie. She gives me a confused look. The tea hasn't finished steeping.

"What? Why?"

"Frank's in the hospital."

Her face pales, and she looks like she's about to pass out. Wordlessly, she heads toward the door and grabs her car keys from a hook on the wall. I follow her out the door and into her car.

*

"When do we get to see him?"

"I'm sorry, ma'am. You can't see him right now."

He was allegedly alert when we got the call. While speeding on the highway to the hospital, I learned that he has gone into cardiac arrest. Right now, I'm seated in a hallway near the emergency room while Natalie is standing up talking to a nurse. We're both nervous, antsy, sweating through our clothes. This all happened suddenly. My heart hurts and my lungs feel tight, like I can't take in a deep enough breath.

"I'm his fiancé. Please, we have to talk—"

"He won't be able to speak, ma'am, even if you go into the room. His blood pressure is critically low, and we're working hard to keep his heart pumping. Please, sit down. I'll come back with an update as soon as there's a change in his condition."

"Okay, okay." Natalie holds her hands over her face as she cries. Slowly, she makes her way to the seat next to mine and slumps down in the chair, shoulders shaking with her sobs.

"I'm sorry," I say, pulling her into a side-hug. I should be crying, but I'm not. For some reason, seeing Natalie heartbroken is enough to send me into a protective, calm state. When Mom died, I had no one to comfort, so I was the one locking myself in a bathroom and crying my eyes out, so no one would notice a grown man losing it at the loss of his mother.

"He'll live, won't he?" she asks between hiccups, rubbing viciously at her face. "He'll live. He has to."

"I don't know," I whisper, uncertain. "God, I hope he lives. But look, it'll be okay. It'll all be okay."

The nurse walks over to us, sober in expression.

"Mr. Whitmer, Ms. Green, I'm sorry. We lost Frank."

And just like that, the world I know is gone. No one will eat those ribs tonight.

When we're let in, they've cleaned up a little. It's painful, looking at Frank's cold, white corpse.

How did this happen to you? Just an hour and a half ago, we were joking together, having fun at your house, talking about you, your upcoming wedding. Maybe it wasn't all optimistic chatter, but we wanted you to be happy. That's what we wanted, Natalie and I. But what we wanted then didn't come. What we have is this: a soulless vessel.

I hold Dad's hand as I sit beside the bed on a creaky plastic chair. "I'm sorry, Dad."

It feels like I jinxed it, by telling him to drive carefully.

We're informed by a police officer that he rear-ended a truck while going 78 MPH in a 65 zone. It was his fault. We can't sue the trucker. We have the option to salvage the car for parts, but it's mostly destroyed.

The day finishes at a rapid pace, mainly because I can't remember most of it.

Tonight, the same night of the crash, I lay in bed with Natalie. It isn't romantic or sexual, but we're both exhausted, and neither of us can stand the idea of sleeping alone tonight. We keep space between us, we turn back-to-back and quietly mourn in the dark. I don't think she sleeps. I scarcely shut my eyes.

Chapter 19: Heaven Is A Woman

After the funeral, I moved into the mansion. I inherited it, and it feels empty with just the two of us. Natalie's here, and she hasn't gone to a single interview for the charity since the accident. She's seeing a therapist to help treat her recently developed agoraphobia.

"Marlon, would you like me to cut up that watermelon in the fridge?"

"Sure, that sounds great."

I'm thankful that Mariah's left the workplace. That makes life easier, now that I've had to deal with the aftermath of Dad's death. I have too much stuff now, since I was Dad's only son. He hadn't added Natalie to the will, but I know that he would have wanted Natalie to have everything special to him. I transferred half his money to her, I consider this house half hers, but really, we share everything in equal parts. We have our own personal spaces, and Natalie has been spending a great deal of time in her art room, planning for her charity, and mourning Dad through her artwork.

The thing is, we've been mourning him for three months now. It's weird living here, but I've started to like it recently. Natalie is working on stepping outside, first in the backyard, and now she can make it to the street without freaking out.

And whenever she's anxious, I hold her close to me, have her feel my steady heartbeat.

We abstained from each other for the first month. By the second month, we were kissing, and she told me she wanted to make it official. We quietly married, holding the whole ceremony at this house — it's big enough for that function — and we were snubbed by a few relatives who disagreed with how fast we got together after Dad's death.

But they don't understand us.

Natalie brings over the sliced watermelon and sits beside me on the couch in the living room.

"Thanks, honey." I kiss her after taking a bite of sweet, seedless melon. She giggles and puts her bare feet up on the couch, draping her legs over mine.

"Of course, baby," she says smiling.

We've been helping each other heal. It took a while, but we're comfortable now. We're comfortable loving each other. Frank would have wanted us to be happy. I know that in my heart, and so does Natalie. We were meant for each other, and maybe it's crazy, or wrong of me to think this, but I feel like Dad's death meant something. I'm not happy that he died, don't get me wrong. But he died with optimism in his heart, that he would be with Natalie. He died loved. And his death opened up the space for more love to grow, love that will last longer than he would have been around.

"Put that watermelon down, honey."

She sets the tray on a side table. "Why?" she asks cutely, fluttering her long eyelashes at me.

I take her by the ankles and place her legs over my shoulders, crawling on top of her so my face is over hers. I take in her beauty, and when I press our lips together, I can taste her sweetness. It's not just the watermelon.

"What's gotten into you, Marlon?"

My kisses trace her jaw to her ear. She unbuttons her blouse and reveals her braless chest. I suck her nipples, which get hard fast, and I listen to the music of her excited breath, feel the staggered rise and fall of her chest. My hands trace her naked torso, cupping her breasts, sliding down to her butt, tracing her thighs from the outside then in.

I cup her and kiss her deeply, loving every sensation that comes from being with the love of my life.

"You, Natalie. You got inside me, remember?"

She takes her skirt off for me. I help her remove her panties. I slip inside of her, and it feels like heaven. We move against each other, and I'm very careful with how I touch her belly.

We're going to be parents, living in a mansion, raising our child as a couple. We were meant to be together. I was meant to put that golden ring on her finger. I trust her fully, and with her I've lost my insecurities. With me, she's found endless support and infinite affection.

Our love is sincere, simple, pure. We live, for what it's worth.

9 798201 250942